Stitch in the Ditch

Mibs Monahan Mysteries #3

By Joan L. Kelly

Full Quiver Publishing,
Pakenham ON

Stitch in the Ditch (Mibs Monahan Mysteries #3)
Copyright 2023 Joan L. Kelly

Published by
Full Quiver Publishing
PO Box 244
Pakenham, Ontario K0A 2X0
www.fullquiverpublishing.com

ISBN Number: 978-1-987970-52-4
Printed and bound in the USA
Cover design: James Hrkach
Cover model: Evelina Zhu

NATIONAL LIBRARY OF CANADA
CATALOGUING IN PUBLICATION

Published by FQ Publishing

A Division of Innate Productions

This book is dedicated to my beautiful,
talented, and caring daughters.
You make your mother proud.
It is also dedicated to my parents,
who taught me to love God, love my family,
and love my country.

Chapter 1

As he approached the deserted lot, the driver turned off his headlights and removed his foot from the gas, tapping the brakes to slow down the car as he made a quick right turn. The crunch of gravel and the engine's low hum were the only sounds breaking the silence as the vehicle slid under the branches of a tree and came to a halt at the darkened corner of the lot. The man looked around carefully, checking both his side mirrors and the rear-view mirror before he turned, placed his arm on the back of the seat, and swiveled his head from side to side. No one should be here, but he remained cautious.

The dark-clothed character clicked off the overhead light before he opened the car door and slid out. He circled around the lot until he was close to the back door. With one more careful scan, he moved up to the entrance. Then, using the light emitted by the wire-enclosed security bulb, the man inserted a key to gain access and swiftly slid into the building.

Twice before, these middle-of-the-night visits had been successful. Removing the valuable antiques and replacing them with carefully crafted forgeries had netted the man a tidy sum. This last switch should provide the financial buffer that would allow him to slink away from this town and live in a more luxurious style.

His patience had been stretched to the breaking point at this small but popular museum. The job at the Gregory Tuppence Museum required the employee to spend his workday in various areas of the building. Despite his college degree, he felt like little more than a glorified gofer. Besides, he was much brighter than the manager or curator. The museum's other employees didn't seem to have the ambition and drive that he possessed. His inconsequential coworkers were content with the menial work assignments dished out each week. But not him. No. *He* was meant for bigger things.

He knew or could easily research each item's estimated value when pulled out of a crate, then taken to the shelves and display cases. He believed himself worth much more than the meager salary deposited into his checking account each week. Moving toward the jewelry display room, the man reasoned, 'This switch tonight will help even things out.'

Instead of wasting his time in this small town, he could be doing much more. The daily visitors meant nothing to him. The majority of the locals were beneath him. Those with the money and power that his egotistical mind considered worth his attention were few and far between in Havendale. The late Gregory Tuppence, for example, was a man of money, power, and influence. His life-long collection of art and antiquities, along with his mansion, had been bequeathed to the town. But the majority of the other small-town citizens didn't interest him.

He'd copied several keys, which he'd 'borrowed' from Catherine Kind's desk. With gloved hands, he pulled out one of those keys and used it to open a glass-topped display. He deliberately and carefully lifted out a piece of antique jewelry, slipped it into his left pocket, and replaced it with a duplicate one from his right. Closing and relocking the case, he moved to the weapons room. He'd just reached the wall, which held the Toledo steel dagger with its inlaid gold and silver handle when the overhead light snapped on. Spinning around to face the person standing inside the door with his hand still on the light switch, the forger froze.

"It's you," the museum's curator, Roger Patterson, said, recognizing him. "I can't believe it! I had reluctantly begun to suspect Joe, the security guard. That was only because he used to be a jeweler. I couldn't think of anyone else who would have the skills to reproduce the ruby necklace that I suspect has been replaced with a fake."

"Hmph," the thief sneered. "I didn't even cross your mind. Did I?" He puffed his chest out and stepped closer to Patterson. "Everyone here underestimates me. It's like they just stare through me." Glaring at the curator, he questioned, "How did you discover that the necklace was a forgery?"

"I make it a point once a week to pick out a room and view each item in that area. After all these years, I can recognize every piece and know where each belongs. Two weeks ago, I went through the jewelry." Shaking his head, Patterson said, "Even though the necklace now on display is beautiful, I could tell something was different. So I removed it from the case and studied it with my jeweler's loupe and then the dichroscope. It is a good forgery, but it's still a forgery. I've contacted the insurance company. I'm waiting for them to call me back about sending an appraiser to check the entire collection."

"Why are you here tonight?" He gave Patterson a suspicious leer. "Why haven't you called in the police yet?"

"Because I suspected Joe Craton, a man I've known and respected for years, and I wanted to make sure. If it were him, I would have been disappointed, but I would have had no choice but to call the authorities." The curator pulled out his phone. "I suspected that the thief came the day after the monthly cleaning because the newly dusted displays would be less likely to show any smudges or disturbance."

With a loud sigh, Roger Patterson lifted his phone and hit the first button to call the police. The thief moved quickly, reaching the curator in a fraction of a second.

Patterson gasped, and his eyes widened as a dagger pierced his chest.

The assailant had plunged with enough force to bury the Toledo steel dagger all the way up to the handle. He pulled the knife out.

Patterson slumped to the ground, dead.

The crook stared at the blood dripping from the weapon. Killing had never been in his plans. But it was too late to undo what was done. Somewhat surprised by his lack of remorse, he stared down at the dead body at his feet. "Well, what do I do now?" He noticed the neatly folded handkerchief, which edged the pocket of Patterson's shirt, and he saw a splatter of blood tinging the white material. He pulled out the handkerchief and used it to wipe down the dagger blade. "I guess I can't switch this knife now since it will still hold traces of blood. But I don't want to take it home. Hmm."

He scanned the wall where various antique blades hung. Noticing an anelace, a medieval long dagger, in a decorative sheath, he decided that the hilt was about the same size as the dagger's handle in his hand. After grabbing a chair from the hallway, he stepped up and pulled the anelace from its casing, replacing it with the shorter dagger. The sheath was sixteen inches long, much longer than needed for the shorter knife, but the hilt held the blade securely in place. He smiled and stepped down. He figured that Patterson was probably the only one who would notice the difference. Peering down at the deceased curator, the forger realized that he no longer needed to worry about that man seeing anything ever again.

The thief, now a murderer, held the long knife in one hand and the bloody cloth in the other. Patterson had suspected Craton because of his knowledge of jewelry. Maybe he could use that fact to his advantage. Making his way to the back of the museum, the killer located the sweater that the old, gray-haired security guard occasionally wore on chilly days. He stuffed the handkerchief deep into the sweater's pocket. He knew exactly where to place the anelace dagger. A new shipment had come in recently and was not yet unpacked. Opening a crate in the back area of the museum, he slipped it in among the various items inside.

Patting his pocket, he felt the shape of the stolen brooch. Even without the antique dagger, he would have enough for his planned move. He nodded. His contriving mind reasoned that he could use the curator's death as a good excuse to quit. No one would question a guy who wanted to leave a place of employment where a murder occurred. As he went back to the front of the museum, the intruder stopped long enough to return the chair to the hallway before heading to the back exit. He left without a backward glance, exiting the same door he'd previously come in and making sure it locked.

Chapter 2

Lieutenant Jace Trueblood guided his ocean-blue Chevy Silverado into a parking spot at the Gregory Tuppence Museum. He hadn't bothered to unload the step ladder, hedge shears, and other supplies from the truck bed. The call from dispatch had come just as Jace pulled into his driveway after visiting the hardware store. He usually worked on Tuesdays but had taken the day off to get some outside work done before the weather got too cold. Jace had quickly changed from his jeans and sweatshirt into a suit, his typical attire worn as the Chief of Detectives, and hurried over to the crime scene. His team had reached the building a few minutes before him. Detectives Mendoza and Clearwater were near the front entrance, slipping on paper booties and plastic gloves.

~~

Juan Mendoza watched as the lieutenant stepped out of his truck and adjusted his tie. Besides being his boss, Jace had become one of Juan's best friends. At 6'3", the broad-shouldered, chestnut-haired, blue-eyed Trueblood was considered handsome by many. Two years ago, when he transferred to Havendale from a Nashville, Tennessee police force, the attractive thirty-one-year-old had unofficially been placed on the town gossips' list of most eligible bachelors. Not many months after that, to the regret of several single young women in the area, his name was removed from the daters' roll when he fell utterly, head-over-heels in love. The seasoned detective usually kept a professional, no-nonsense attitude with most people, facing down hardened criminals and eliciting fear from those on the other side of the table in an interrogation room. However, when a certain red-haired, green-eyed young lady smiled at him, his breath caught, and his heart melted. Juan knew that the sweet but strong-willed seamstress, Mirabelle Monahan, had similar feelings for Jace Trueblood.

~~

A few months ago, Jace almost lost Mibs. She was the only witness able to identify a shooter who had killed a man at the local community theater. The murderer nearly succeeded in eliminating Mibs as a witness when he brutally stabbed her. Jace and Aunt Bernie, the girl's octogenarian great-aunt, along with several friends, waited anxiously for hours as Mibs hovered between life and death in the hospital's intensive care unit. The realization that he may lose the girl who had captured his heart had sent Jace to his knees, asking God to please let her wake up and stay with him. His prayer was answered, and six weeks later, Jace put a diamond ring on Mibs' finger, asking her to spend the rest of her life with him.

"Lieutenant," Detective Mendoza, the brown-eyed Mexican American, Trueblood's second in command in the field, said, "We were just heading in to see the body. Officer Schroeder was the first on the scene. She escorted the employees to their break room, watching where they were walking and ensuring they didn't touch anything. Clarkson cordoned off the murder scene and is guarding the area."

Trueblood acknowledged the information with a nod. Accepting the requisite shoe covers, he asked, "Do we know the victim's name?"

Detective Eve Clearwater, a recent transfer to the Havendale Detective Division, answered, "Roger Patterson. He's been the curator since this building was turned into a museum ten years ago, right after Gregory Tuppence bequeathed it to the people of Havendale." Entering the building with the others, she added, "My understanding is that he's been stabbed."

"We've called the medical examiner and the crime scene technicians," Mendoza said. "Gene Delgado is at the station pulling up information on Patterson's family, friends, and background. I'd be surprised if we find anything unexpected about him since he's been a member of the community for years."

"Does it appear to be a robbery gone wrong?"

Mendoza shrugged. "We haven't been able to determine that yet."

"Juan, do you know who the next of kin is? We'll want to notify them before they hear it on the news or through the local grapevine, which is sometimes even faster."

"I believe he had a wife and several grown children. If Delgado doesn't already have the wife's name, Catherine Kind, the manager, is here. She should know."

Jace had been in Havendale for over two years now but had never visited this local museum. He scanned the entrance hall as they headed for the area with the deceased Patterson's body, noting the array of artwork and pricey objects on display. When Jace entered the weapons room, he nodded to Brett Clarkson, a uniformed policeman with smooth, coffee-colored skin and a lean build. Clarkson stepped aside, allowing the detective to view the body.

"Who all has been in here?" Trueblood asked.

"Besides me," answered Clarkson, "Officer Schroeder and the manager, Catherine Kind. She's the one who found the body. Also, Robert Jackson, the janitor. To my knowledge, that's all. At least since Schroeder and I arrived."

Lieutenant Trueblood stood over the dead man, letting his eyes rove across the body and the surrounding hardwood floor. "Clarkson, was that footprint there when you came in?" He indicated a bloody print near Patterson's shoulder.

"Yes, sir. The janitor said he'd bent down to make sure Roger Patterson was dead. So I checked the print with his shoe; it matched. He left a couple smudges as he walked away. I placed a marker by each of them." Then, pointing to another smear of blood near the body, Clarkson added, "That area is too smudged to determine if it was also made by Jackson." His brow furrowed in concentration. "I think it was made earlier because of the dryer edges."

Pulling out a small, soft-sided book from his

pocket, Jace filled in a page with notes. As he squatted down to get a closer view, the detective studied the victim and the drying blood pooled around his shoulder and side. "How soon before the crime scene technicians get here?"

"Benson and his team should be here within the next few minutes," Clearwater said.

Jace stood up and slowly surveyed the room. From the initial examination, it did appear that Patterson had been stabbed. They were standing in a display room full of weapons, so the killer wouldn't have had to bring a weapon with him. There were plenty to choose from quickly at hand. However, it was just as likely that the attacker had brought a knife and took it with him when leaving.

"Mendoza, start searching for anything that seems suspicious, especially missing knives or blood spots anywhere. You know what to look for." He turned to the other detective. "Detective Clearwater, let's go talk to Ms. Kind and the other employees."

Jace found Officer Schroeder in a back room, watching over the employees. The Gregory Tuppence Museum manager sat at an oval table, her hands twisting together. Sitting near her were two employees, a plump, doe-eyed woman who appeared to be in her late twenties and a young man wearing a pocket patch embroidered with the name Bob. The woman had her arm around Catherine Kind, patting her shoulder. The middle-aged manager was obviously shaken from finding Patterson.

"Ms. Kind?" Trueblood asked.

"Yes, and it's Mrs. Kind," she corrected softly.

"Yes, ma'am," he responded. "I'm Lieutenant Jace Trueblood, and this is Detective Eve Clearwater. We'd like to ask you some questions."

"Of course. Whatever you need." Her voice sounded strained.

Jace indicated the other two people. "Are these the only employees?"

"No," Kind answered. "The security guard, Joe Craton, comes in at 9:30, half an hour before we open. The two art handlers, Albert Borne and Nick Mosely, work from 10:00 to 5:00, and Patrick Clyde is our other part-time help. He works Fridays and Saturdays. We're closed on Sundays and Mondays." With a lifted hand, she introduced the two employees already present. "This is Nancy Bloom; she handles the small souvenir counter, helps customers, and does anything else that needs to be done while she is here on Tuesday through Thursday. Bob Jackson is our janitor. Bob comes in each morning at 8:30, the same time I'm scheduled to come in. But I often come in a little early." Catherine Kind bit down on her lower lip as tears welled in her eyes. "Like today, I was ten minutes early. I...I went to the office first, like normal, put away my jacket and purse, grabbed the keys from my desk, and started my usual walk-through." The furrows on her forehead deepened, and she seemed to sway.

Nancy Bloom put her arm back around the older woman. "It's all right, Cathy. It's going to be all right," she said.

Eve Clearwater reached for a paper cup from a stack sitting on the counter and filled it from the faucet. "Here, Mrs. Kind, would you like a sip of water before you continue?"

The distraught manager accepted the drink, swallowed, then said, "Thank you." The woman sat a little straighter and took a deep breath. "What do you want to know, Detective Trueblood?"

"Please continue with what you were telling us. You started through the building...."

She nodded. "Yes. It's how I start each day. I'm not really expecting anything to actually be wrong. We've never had a serious problem. But, occasionally, someone will leave a dust cloth out, or a picture may be hanging the littlest bit crooked. I just want everything to be nice for our visitors." Releasing a deep sigh, Mrs. Kind continued, "I turn the lights on as I enter each display room. As soon as I walked into...that room, I saw him...I saw Roger on the floor. I thought that he may have had a heart attack or stroke. Then I saw the blood." She stopped talking and shuddered. "I froze, couldn't move. I think maybe I screamed."

"She did scream," Bob Jackson, a young man in his early twenties, tall and rail-thin, said. "I came in the back; it must have been about twenty-five after eight. I had just shut the door behind me when I heard Mrs. Kind; she sounded terrified. I found her standing over the body, hands over her mouth. I thought she would get sick, so I moved her aside to check the victim," the young janitor explained. "I couldn't find a pulse." Then, taking a quick breath, he added, "I was sure Mr. Patterson was dead, and I called 911."

"Did you come to this room then?"

Jackson shook his head. "No, we went to Mrs. Kind's office. That's actually where I dialed the emergency number. I used her desk phone."

Trueblood addressed the other employee. "When did you come in, Ms. Bloom?"

"I arrived a little after 8:30. I don't usually come to work until 9:00, but I planned on leaving a little early today. Mrs. Kind had approved of me adjusting my schedule," she explained. "As I got out of my van, I heard sirens. I'd almost reached the building when a police car pulled into the lot, followed by an ambulance. I saw a police officer try to open the front door. As soon as the officer realized it was locked, she turned to me." Nancy Bloom removed her arm from Mrs. Kind and crossed her arms around herself as if trying to ward off the memory. "She..." Bloom nodded toward Officer Schroeder. "...asked me if I had a key. I nodded and handed her the key to the back door. She and the other officer ran around back. Then, a few minutes later, the front door opened, and the EMTs hurried in." Hesitating for a moment, Bloom scanned the faces of the two detectives. "No one had told me what was going on, so I followed them inside. I heard Cathy's – Mrs. Kind's – voice coming from her office, so I headed there. She and Bob told me about Mr. Patterson. A moment later, the policewoman asked if we had a room to sit and wait, so we followed her back here to the break area."

Jace scrutinized the three employees, shattered expressions prominent on their faces.

"Mrs. Kind, could you supply the name of Roger Patterson's closest relative? It would probably be good to contact them."

"Oh my. Poor Linda." Catherine Kind put her hands over her mouth and moaned for a moment before standing. "Yes, if I can go back to my office. I have Roger's address and his wife's cell phone number."

"Detective Clearwater, go with her. Mrs. Kind, please be careful not to disturb anything while getting the address." Jace glanced at his detective for a moment.

~~

Eve had only been part of the Havendale Detective Division for a few months, so Jace was still learning what on-the-job skills she possessed. So far, he was impressed with her abilities both at the station, behind the computer, and in the field. Jace had taken his newest detective out for coffee the first week she started. He liked to get to know his team, especially anyone new. In fact, he occasionally tried to take a break with each team member. The lead detective felt that giving the men and women a chance to talk one-on-one with him kept an open work relationship. Any concerns could be corrected before they became problems.

Jace learned that Evening Star Clearwater had grown up in Arizona. Detective Clearwater was two-thirds Native American, mainly of Navaho heritage. Her brown eyes were accented by high cheekbones and dark hair. Eve possessed a calm, attentive manner that served well in her line of work. As they drank their coffee and talked, Jace liked what he saw in the detective's personality. They even brought up the less-than-common names they both possessed. Jace explained that his last name was Celtic, originating from Ireland and Southern England regions. He also explained that his first name, Jace, came from his two grandfathers' names. Both his dad's father and his mom's father had hinted that they would be pleased if the firstborn son were named after him. So, rather than disappoint either man, Jace's mom and dad had combined the first two letters of each name – James and Cecil – telling his two grandfathers that he was named after both of them.

Jace had smiled to himself as he shared that story with Eve, remembering when he'd given that same information to Mibs. Several months ago, Jace teasingly told his girlfriend he'd tell her the origin of his first name if she would explain why her childhood friend, Tony Vitali, occasionally called her by the nickname, *Wonderful.*

~~

Stepping closer to Detective Clearwater, Jace quietly asked, "Eve, have you done many family death notifications before? Would you be good

getting the address and taking care of that?”
Talking to a victim’s family was never easy.
Clearwater responded, “I’ve had that unpleasant responsibility before. It’s not my favorite part of the job, but I can handle it.”
“Okay. Take Clarkson with you,” he said.

Chapter 3

Lieutenant Trueblood finished gathering information from Nancy Bloom and Bob Jackson just as Delgado arrived. "You two can go home for now," the lieutenant addressed the two employees. "We may need to talk to both of you later. Please remain available." He motioned toward Schroeder. "This officer will escort you out."

Turning to Mrs. Kind, who had been brought back to the room, Jace checked his notes and said, "I have down that Joe Craton gets here at 9:30 and the art handlers, Borne and Mosely, at 10:00. According to the clock, Craton should be here soon and the others shortly after."

"Yes, that's correct," she replied.

"Detective Delgado," Jace said, "head out to the parking lot and watch for those men. I don't want them to see the police presence outside and leave." Stopping the detective, Trueblood added, "Unless you found something of vital importance about the deceased, you can fill me in on any details about Roger Patterson after interviews are done. Take Craton to the station and start interviewing him. Have an officer meet you there with the other two. Use your judgment; unless you feel there is a reason to hold them, send them home after their interview."

Delgado nodded. "Yes, Lieutenant."

Jace turned to the museum manager. "Do you know if your other employee..." Jace rechecked his notes. "…Patrick Clyde would be available today if we called him?"

Mrs. Kind shook her head, her face drawn and pale. "Patrick is a student finishing up his degree. He's probably in class at the university right now."

"Let's return to your office, check the records, and get his contact information," Jace instructed. "I'll have someone see if they can reach him."

As the woman flipped through her files in the office, Jace pulled out a chair and sat down. After Kind gave him the address and phone number of the part-time employee, he called the desk sergeant at the station and passed on the information.

"Mrs. Kind, I know you've had quite a shock, but I need your help," Jace requested.

Catherine Kind hesitated for a moment before squaring her shoulders. "How can I help?"

"First, I need a list of anyone who has a key to the building."

"Oh, well, that's easy enough," the manager replied. "I have one, and Mr. Patterson has…" she hesitated. "…had one. Joe Craton, the security guard, has a key, as does Nancy Bloom. Also, I keep a spare in the top drawer of my desk."

"Okay." Jace wrote the information down as he thought about the number of keys floating around. "Next, although nothing at first glance appears to be missing, I need a complete inventory done. With so many valuable items stored in this museum, there may be something that isn't in its place, something not easily missed."

Mrs. Kind dried her eyes and blew her nose before answering. "Of course, Detective Trueblood, I will start right away. It will go more quickly if I have help. Could I call Nancy back in or have the art handlers, Albert and Nick, assist?"

"No, none of the employees. But I'll have someone from the police department help you. You can supervise the process."

"Why can't an employee help?"

"There is no indication of forced entry into the building. My team has already checked the doors and windows. It would appear that the attacker either entered with Mr. Patterson or had a key to let themselves in."

The wide-eyed manager stared at the lawman. "Are you saying that you think someone from the museum did this?"

"Not necessarily, but we haven't eliminated anyone yet," he said.

Trueblood moved the chair back and stood up. The manager nervously wrung her hands together again. With a soft voice, hoping to calm her frazzled nerves, Jace said, "Thank you, Mrs. Kind. You've been very accommodating."

"You're welcome, Detective Trueblood." she tried to put on a brave face. She opened her laptop. "I'll pull up the inventory list right now."

Stopping just outside the manager's door, the lieutenant scanned the hall. Martha Schroeder was talking to another officer. He called to her.

"Officer Schroeder, will you stay with Mrs. Kind until I send someone from the station to help her with the inventory?"

Schroeder nodded, quickly stepped forward, and stationed herself inside the office.

Continuing on to the weapon display area, Jace found the crime scene specialists processing the murder scene.

"Todd," Jace greeted lead technician Todd Benson, head of the local CSI team.

When someone meets Todd Benson for the first time, they see a grandfatherly type. He is soft-spoken with gray eyes and wire-rimmed glasses. Underneath the calm exterior rests a sharp mind and keen eyes. Benson often picked up subtle clues that less observant people missed.

"Hello, Lieutenant," Todd responded. Jerking his head toward the stretcher being used to transport the victim, he said, "I gave them the okay to take the deceased to the morgue. We already have pictures and notes. Dr. Duffy, the new medical examiner, just left after a preliminary exam; she'll let us know if she finds anything significant." Benson handed Jace his notes. "Duffy said that it appears the weapon used was a dagger, estimated to be six to eight inches long, with one smooth edge and one serrated. The hilt is four inches in width and has tapered ends."

"How can she be so sure about the width of the dagger's handle?"

"According to Duffy, the blade had been driven all the way in, all the way up to the hilt. Patterson's shirt was thin enough that it didn't stop the force used from leaving an impression." Benson motioned to his photographer. "Samuel, please show Lieutenant Trueblood the picture of the bruising on the victim's chest."

Jace studied the photo, noting the faintly visible bruise extending on either side of the stab wound.

Benson pointed. "You can see not only the length of the dagger's handle but other details. It appears to be some type of open-work design."

Scanning the daggers displayed across one of the walls, Jace saw several that seemed to match the description. "The killer probably took the weapon with him or her, but in case they didn't, we need to check any dagger that fits the report."

"Figured you'd say that," Benson responded. "I'm going to use a high-intensity light to search for any indications of blood. Samuel has an infrared film that helps document blood stains on dark surfaces." With a puckered mouth, he added, "I prefer not to use luminol on small areas except as a last resort. I've found that it can dilute or smear blood impressions, and the chemical reaction has the potential to destroy a few types of evidence."

Jace gave an approving nod. "You know your job, Todd. Do what's needed. I'll check back with you before you leave."

Jace slowly ran his eyes across the dagger display wall, marking down notes of any knife that fit the general description of the murder weapon. Two had hilts with pointed ends and ornamental open-work; those should be given special attention. He scanned the adjourning wall, devoted mainly to swords. The detective noticed three daggers displayed as part of matching sets. Although the attentive technician, Benson, would most certainly see them, Jace would still follow up. He believed in double-checking things, especially in a murder investigation.

Jace had just finished when Officer Keil Harte stepped into the room.

"Lieutenant," he called. "Detective Mendoza found something. He'd like you to come to the back of the building."

Jace followed Harte to a small area past the break room. A set of lockers were attached to the wall, and coat hooks were secured under each locker. As Jace approached, Juan Mendoza pointed to a gray wool sweater. An officer stood nearby holding a video camera, documenting the search.

"What do you have, Juan?"

Mendoza pulled a stained handkerchief the rest of the way out of a pocket of the gray sweater, then turned to his boss. "As soon as I found this cloth, I saw the blood."

"Do we know whose sweater this is?" Jace asked.

Mendoza pointed to a name card taped to the locker above. "Appears to belong to someone named Joe Craton."

"Craton?" Jace repeated. "Joe Craton is headed to the station with Delgado."

Jace left the others to log the evidence as he headed back to the Havendale Police Station. Once there, he watched through a two-way mirror for several minutes while Delgado proceeded with routine questions. When the questioning seemed to be nearing an end, Jace tapped on the door, entered the room, and sat next to the other detective.

Jace studied the older man. He had dozens of interviews and cross-examinations under his belt and had a better-than-average instinct about when a person was hiding something. After talking with Joe Craton for a few minutes, he felt little likelihood that this aged security guard was guilty of murder. However, he'd met some criminals who were so skilled at lying that they could have pursued successful careers as actors.

"So, you don't know how this blood-stained handkerchief ended up in the pocket of your sweater, Mr. Craton?" Jace asked, showing Craton the picture on his cell phone.

The suspect's shoulders slumped, and a bewildered expression settled on his face. "I have no idea. This picture is of my sweater. I leave it hanging on that hook whenever I don't need it, so anyone could have slipped something into the pocket."

Jace left the interview room and stepped into the hall to have a discussion with Sergeant Brice Long. Long's ability to coordinate things was the main reason activities ran smoothly inside the Havendale detective unit. Jace often used him as a sounding board.

"I don't think Craton has anything to do with the stabbing," Jace told Brice. "I'm going to let him go with the notice that he's still under suspicion."

Sergeant Long nodded. "I'll find someone to drive him back to his car."

"Brice, let one of the office staff handle that and have someone cover your desk. I want you to come with me," Jace instructed.

Chapter 4

Jace returned to the crime scene, bringing Sergeant Long with him. He introduced Long to Mrs. Kind, assuring her that the sergeant would be more than adequate help for a thorough inventory.

As the lieutenant made his way back to the weapons room, his phone rang. Seeing the caller's name, he smiled as he answered. "Hi, sweetheart."

"Hi, honey," Mibs answered. "You mentioned that you were working at your house today, so I thought I'd see if you wanted me to bring lunch over."

"Well, things didn't go as planned," he replied. "There's been a homicide, and I'm at the scene now."

"Oh, no!" Mibs paused. "Was it anyone I know? Or can you tell me?"

"If you'd called a few minutes ago, I would have said no. The family has now been notified, and a news van has already pulled into the lot. Since it's becoming public knowledge anyway, I can tell you it was Roger Patterson, the curator at the museum." Jace paused. "Did you know him?"

"I've seen him a few times, but he was only a casual acquaintance."

"Hmm," Jace mumbled. As he stepped into the display room doorway, he watched the CSI team intently going over the area. "Mibs, there is something you could do, if you don't mind."

"Sure, if I can. What do you need?"

"If I call in an order to Blueberry Grove Café, would you pick it up and bring it over? I've got a crew working here, and they'll probably be hungry by lunchtime."

"Of course. I'd be glad to do that for you."

"I'll find out what the team wants and have it ordered for curbside pick-up by 12:30," Jace instructed. "Oh, and Mibs, be sure and call when you get here. I can't have food brought into the crime scene. The officers and technicians can come out and take a break in my truck or one of the squad cars."

"Okay. See you in a while, Jace."

"Thanks, Mibs."

~~

Around 1:00 p.m., the officers at the site and the other team members took turns stepping outside to grab a sandwich and drink. Mibs had shoved the items in the bed of Jace's truck forward and used the back end as a makeshift tail-gate picnic area for the crew.

Detective Mendoza seemed to be the last one to take a break. When Juan finished his lunch, Mibs asked him if Jace might come out.

"He's so focused on the investigation, I doubt if he realizes what time it is." Juan scrunched up the wrapper from his sub and tossed it into the trash bag. "Let me escort you to the break room in the back of the building. Then, I'll tell Jace you're waiting for him. That should get his attention and force him to take a break."

Mibs paced around the break area for a while, finally stopping at a window and watching the wind weave through the last few autumn leaves, making them dance as they stubbornly clung to a nearby maple tree. Hearing her name, she turned and felt her heart skip when she saw the smile on her fiancé's face.

"Hi, Mibs." Jace walked toward her. "Thanks for bringing lunch for the team."

"You're welcome, honey." Mibs stepped up to meet him. "Why don't you come out and have a sandwich?"

"In a few minutes. I want to see them finish checking the last few knives on the dagger wall. Despite a large number of knives, the forensic team has found only very minute, ancient traces of blood on a couple of them, no recent samples."

Sighing and shaking her head, Mibs didn't try to argue with him. "At least make sure you stop to get something to drink every so often."

~~

"Okay, boss," he teased her. Then, reaching for Mibs' hand, he tilted his head and peered into her sparkling green eyes. Instead of reading social media or posting online comments, Jace knew that Mibs preferred to use her free time reading or working on word searches, cryptograms, and other brain games. The detective called to mind a previous crime scene when this spirited seamstress had pointed out a thread of evidence and another time when she located a missing slug from a bullet, which helped solve a murder.

"I was just thinking, Mibs. There've been a couple times when you pointed out evidence that hadn't been found by anyone else." He ran his hand through his curly hair and thought for a moment before speaking again. "Would you like to be a consultant for a few minutes? You could come into the weapons room, but don't touch anything. Just see if anything seems out of place. Maybe your propensity for solving puzzles could be useful."

With a shrug, she accepted the challenge. "All right."

They reached the area still occupied by CSI personnel. Jace pointed to a table the forensic team had set up. Several daggers were being studied by the investigators. Jace picked up an ornately designed knife, which had already been examined and dusted for prints. "Mibs, this is the type and size of the dagger that the M.E. said was used to stab the curator, Patterson. I figure the killer took the actual weapon when they left, but we're still checkin' any knife that fits the description."

Mibs carefully studied the knife. "This hilt is very intricate; it has a beautiful filigree design."

"What do you mean by the word *filigree*?" Jace thought he knew but wanted her description.

"In this case, filigree is when thin threads or wires, often made of precious metals, are twisted together into a design. This one is a very intricate lace design made of a combination of gold and silver."

"It sure is a beautiful piece of work," Jace commented, "and it's an exact match to the impression of the wound, but there is no trace of blood on it." Waving his hand across the room, he asked, "Okay, my little Nancy Drew, do you see anything that stands out or appears out of place?"

She slowly let her eyes wander across the display walls and leaned forward to intensely study a leather sheath with a knife in it. "The hilt of this dagger has the same design as the one you just showed me."

"I know," Jace said. "I noticed that, but the blade would be too long to match the depth of the wound the medical examiner described. If you notice the placard underneath the sheath, it's described as a 14-inch long knife commonly called an anelace. We'll check all the weapons in this room, but we want to examine the six to eight-inch daggers first."

Mibs studied the other swords and knives on display for a few moments before moving her eyes back to the anelace with the filigree hilt. "It still seems like something is out of place." She turned toward the exhibit area that held only daggers, then back to the long knives. Suddenly, she held up her finger. "I know why something seems wrong."

Jace stepped up next to the intuitive young woman. "What are you thinkin'?" he asked.

"I notice there are several matching weapons, swords, and knives that are obviously parts of sets displayed together at the end of this wall," Mibs observed. "But the anelace and matching dagger are on different walls." Turning her attention back to Jace, she asked, "Why? Why would the curator put all the matching sets together except that one?"

Jace wrinkled his brow and considered her question. He called the lead technician,

Benson. "Todd, please check this short sword next."

The specialist used a step stool to reach the anelace. As soon as he pulled the knife out, he gasped. It wasn't a long knife but rather a seven-inch dagger.

"Of course!" Mibs exclaimed. "*Stitch in the ditch.*"

"What?" Jace asked.

Benson's brows lifted. "Stitch in what?"

"What does a...stitch in the ditch mean?" Jace asked in a perplexed tone.

"Well," she replied, "stitch in the ditch is a sewing term to describe a line of stitches placed along a seam line. The stitching is there, but you won't notice it unless you actually search for it." Seeing the bewilderment on both men's faces, Mibs tried to explain further. "Have you ever read the Edgar Allen Poe story, *The Purloined Letter*?"

Benson slowly nodded.

Jace frowned before answering. "Yes, but it was a long time ago. Didn't it have somethin' to do with the police searchin' for a letter? I believe it was somehow hidden in plain sight."

"Exactly," Mibs agreed. "If I remember correctly, the letter had been turned inside out with a different address written on it, then placed in an easily seen letter holder. Even though the constabulary searched diligently for the letter, they skipped right over it because they expected it to be hidden. I think whoever put that dagger in that sheath tried to use the same ploy."

Jace shook his head and smiled. "Mibs

Monahan, you never cease to amaze me."

Todd Benson carefully carried the dagger to the examining table, where he directed one of his technicians to spread out a clean piece of paper. He set the knife down and used his special light to go over every inch of it. After checking the joint between the hilt and the metal blade, he stopped and took out a long, thin string from a sterile container. Benson ran it along the joint. When he held it up, fresh blood was visible on the collection string.

Turning toward Jace, the chief technician said, "I'll bet a nickel that this will be a match to the victim's blood."

"I think you would win that bet," Jace said. "Todd, I'd like you to personally take that dagger to the lab. Your crew can stay and finish investigating. But before you do, is there anything else that stands out?"

"Hmm," Benson muttered. "The knife we just found is exactly like this other one. I have a feeling it is a copy."

Leaning over to examine it more closely, Jace studied the twin daggers. "They appear to be a matched pair."

Mibs had been standing quietly as Jace and Todd discussed the two knives. Tapping Jace on the shoulder, she pointed to a marred area on each dagger. "Did you notice that even the imperfections are the same? They each have a tiny chip in the blade. Also, the hilts are not just similar but exact. Both have a section of the filigree indented in exactly the same place, and each has a deeply worn spot toward the top." Lifting her eyes to meet Jace's, she said,

"These aren't just simply matched daggers; one is an exact replica, down to the last detail."

Jace straightened, took a breath, let it out, and said, "We obviously have a nearly perfect forgery."

He glanced around to see if Sergeant Long and Mrs. Kind were nearby. But instead, he saw Detective Mendoza passing by the doorway. "Juan," he called as he approached the detective, "can you find Mrs. Kind and bring her in here?"

"I just talked to Sergeant Long," Mendoza answered. "He let Mrs. Kind take a break. I think she's having a bite to eat and a cup of coffee. Do you want me to interrupt her lunch?"

"No, give her a few minutes," Jace said. Then glancing at Mibs, who waited a couple of feet away, he added, "I think someone wants me to take a break." Offering his arm, he smiled when Mibs stepped up to his side. "Did you say there was a sandwich left for me?"

Before he stepped out of the room, he instructed Benson to wait until the museum manager saw the daggers before taking them to the police lab.

~~

When they reached the truck bed, Mibs moved an ice pack in the cooler aside and lifted out a couple sandwiches. "I saved a roast beef and provolone cheese sub for you and a chicken salad on a croissant for me."

"Thanks, Mibs." Jace accepted the sandwich. Grabbing a bottle of water, he suggested they sit inside the truck.

He finished his sub, then tilted his head. He

watched Mibs, a loving expression on his face. "So, have you decided yet?" he asked.

Mibs took the last bite of her sandwich, then wiped her hands and gave him a sideways glance. "Decided what?"

"Have you decided on a date for our wedding?"

"Oh...well..." Mibs laced her fingers together and chewed on her lower lip before answering. "I had been so busy with orders for homecoming dresses and Halloween costumes that I barely had time to think. I haven't even decided on a design for my wedding dress. And," she added, "you're still working on the house. Don't you want time to finish more of it?"

"I finally finished the dining room, which just leaves the rest of the bedrooms and the library. They can be done later. The one thing I do want to get done now is Aunt Bernie's bedroom and bath. I'd love to give her one of the bedroom suites upstairs. I offered to have a chair lift installed for her along the stairway, but she said she'd rather have the downstairs bedroom. I want to make sure it's handicap accessible," Jace replied. "My dad and uncle are making a special trip to Havendale to help me with that project. We can have it done within a couple of weeks. Now that there is this murder to concentrate on, I have a feeling they may be doing most of the remodeling without me."

Scooting a little closer, Jace smiled. "So, should we set a date for a couple weeks from now? As far as I'm concerned, I'd be happy if we got married tomorrow."

Mibs shook her head. "Jace, I can't make my

dress and get everything else ready in two weeks." Mibs paused and sighed; the glint in his eyes indicated that he was teasing her.

He was teasing, but only a little. Jace had told Mibs he didn't want a long engagement. Instead, he was anxious to start their life together as husband and wife.

"What if we get married in the spring? That's a good time for weddings." Mibs waited for a response to her suggestion.

Gathering strands of strawberry hair in his hand, Jace twirled them around his fingers as he gazed at Mibs with tenderness. "I don't want to wait that long." After a moment, he pulled her into his arms. "But I'll do whatever makes you happy."

Mibs' heart beat faster as she realized how much this man tried to bend to her wishes. His willingness to compromise made her love him more. "Jace, this is the end of November, so...how about Valentine's Day? That would give us about ten weeks to take care of items like reserving the church and sending out invitations. I would have time to decide on a wedding dress."

"Valentine's Day," Jace repeated, obviously pleased with her offer. "Okay." He sat back and pulled out his cell phone.

"What are you doing?" Mibs asked.

The edge of his mouth tipped up in a half-smile. "I'm marking the day in my calendar. I don't want anything to interfere with that date." He frowned. "February fourteenth is on a Sunday.

"Oh, I think we both would prefer a Saturday.

What if we make it the thirteenth?" Mibs suggested.

Jace clicked the keys on his phone. "February thirteenth. Good," he said before pulling up his contact list. "I'm calling the rectory to speak with Father Smith."

"Why don't we wait and talk to him after Sunday Mass?"

Jace shrugged. "Valentine's weekend may be a popular time for weddings. I want to make sure we have the day set."

Mibs sat back and smiled as Jace picked up her hand and held it to his heart.

Chapter 5

It was after 2:00 p.m. when Mibs parked behind Monahan's Sewing Shop and entered through the back door, where Shadow greeted her.

Placing the cooler on the floor, she reached down to rub the black-masked Belgian Malinois on the head. "Hello, pretty girl. Did you keep an eye on everything today?"

After greeting the beloved dog, Mibs made her way to the corner where a break area was set up. Carrying two leftover sub sandwiches in her arm, she was glad to find Deanna Maxwell, the morning shift employee, slipping into her coat.

"Deanna," she addressed the good-natured, middle-aged woman, "would you like to take these two sandwiches home to your teenagers? You've mentioned that they have healthy appetites."

"If you don't want them, sure," she readily accepted. "They won't last ten minutes at my house."

"Good! I already have barbeque pork slow cooking in the crockpot for our dinner tonight," Mibs explained as she hung up her jacket. "How did everything go here at the shop while I was gone?"

"We kept busy, sold a lot of the calico cotton you have on sale. Apparently, the ladies' group at one of the local churches has decided to start a quilting club. They plan to make quilts and then sell them to make money for the needy who come to the food pantry."

"That sounds like a good cause," Mibs said. "I'm glad it was on sale when they came. I'll check the inventory and see if we need to replenish our stock of quilting fabrics."

"Oh, I left a message in the order book. A lady came in asking to talk to you about making a christening gown for her grandchild's Baptism. I'd have taken the order and started on it myself, but she asked specifically for Miss Mirabelle Monahan. I told her you'd call her back; I don't know how much time you have left in your schedule. You're already making two costumes for the community theater and planning on starting your own wedding dress."

Mibs blew out a long breath. "I don't think I'll have the time. I will call her back, and I'll suggest that she let you take on the project. Hopefully, I can convey the fact that you are an excellent seamstress and would do a beautiful job."

"Let me know what's decided." Deanna turned toward the rear entrance but stopped. "Mibs, I noticed that you were driving a different car the last few days. Is that just temporary, or did you get a new vehicle?

"I got a different car, a Chevy Impala," Mibs acknowledged. "It isn't new, but it might as well be. My fiancé inherited it from his uncle, who only drove it occasionally and diligently kept it in tip-top shape. Jace and my friend, Tony, went over the whole vehicle to ensure everything was in good order. They changed the oil and other fluids and replaced the belts, hoses, filters, and tires. It's as close to a new car as possible."

"That's nice." Deanna paused before saying, "In that case, I wonder what you'll do with your old car. It appears to still run well. Are you planning on selling it?"

"Actually, I am," Mibs confirmed. "Even though both the Chevy and my Ford are about the same age, my old car has over ninety thousand miles on it. But, on the other hand, the Impala has only been driven twenty-thousand miles. The biggest reason I like the Impala better is because of the extra-large trunk. It's handier for hauling around things for my sewing business."

"I think your old car would work well for my son, Peter, to drive back and forth to school. His dad and I told him we'd match however much he saved for his first car."

"May I ask how much he's saved?"

"He's saved almost five hundred dollars. But we'd cover the difference if the price is reasonable," Deanna assured Mibs.

"You're matching his five hundred. Hmm." Mibs took only a moment to consider the situation. "I've just decided that I'm selling my old car for one thousand dollars." Mibs' eyes sparkled with pleasure. "It's yours if you want it."

Deanna Maxwell gave a short cough. "Miss Monahan...Mibs, your car is in good shape. I'm sure you can get more for it than that. You should check the listed value."

"I don't have to check anything." Mibs

remembered a few months ago when this valuable employee stepped in and practically ran Monahan's Sewing Shop while she was in the hospital. Not to mention the days of recuperation that followed. "I don't know how the shop would have survived if you hadn't taken over the daily routine here when Aunt Bernie and I needed your help. I owe you a lot more than a deal on a used car."

Deanna replied that she was only doing her job. "I would have been without a paycheck if I'd not kept Monahan's doors open."

"We both know it was more than that. In fact…" Mibs hesitated for a moment. "Deanna, can you stay for a couple minutes? I want to discuss something with you."

"Ah, I guess so," she slowly agreed, setting her purse and the subs down on the break table.

"I'll be right back," Mibs said. A few minutes later, she reentered the break area with her business partner, Aunt Bernie. "Please sit down, Deanna. We want to ask you something."

When the trio was situated at the small table, Mibs queried, "Deanna, would you consider becoming the manager of Monahan's Sewing Shop?" Turning to gaze fondly at her beloved aunt, she added, "Aunt Bernie isn't as young as she used to be and needs to be off her feet more. Also, I'm going to have less time to devote to the business while I get ready for my wedding."

Bernie nodded. "It's harder for me to get going in the morning. And I'd like to relax and spend more time visiting my friends. You young people can handle things without much help from me."

The forty-five-year-old mother chuckled. "I'm not used to being called one of the young people."

"Deanna, you did say that now that your kids are all in high school, you could work more hours. Besides, you do most of what a manager would do anyway. It would be full-time and a higher wage." Mibs chewed on her lower lip as she waited for Deanna to answer.

"Thank you for the offer." Deanna drummed her fingers on the tabletop and seemed to be thinking. A wide grin slowly spread across her face. "I accept."

Mibs let out the breath that she hadn't realized she'd been holding. "Great."

Mibs saw relief etched across Aunt Bernie's face. She knew that Aunt Bernie had been a person who believed in setting goals and doing her best to accomplish them. She'd tackled all challenges with determination. Mibs also realized that her aunt's old bones and aching joints were yelling at her to slow down. Since falling and breaking her hip, it became evident that her strength had never fully returned. Mibs suspected that it was just her love and desire to help that kept her going these days.

After Deanna Maxwell left, Bernie went to her room to rest, and Mibs joined Mary Wong, the college student who worked afternoons. The first hour started off slowly, but the last two hours of the day brought a steady stream of customers into the store. Even though Mibs kept busy measuring and cutting material for patrons, she still noted Mary's efficiency.

Mary's knowledge of various materials made her an excellent employee for a fabric and sewing business.

As Monahan's Sewing Shop's owner, Mibs was very pleased with how the young woman could answer almost any question asked about fabrics. Mary could explain the difference between cotton blends, linens, wool fabrics, and various synthetic materials. Mibs had listened to Mary on several occasions as the knowledgeable girl explained various details to customers – damask material is made with a pattern woven into the fabric instead of printed on it, twill had a diagonal rib pattern, and tweed was rough woolen fabric. Since Mibs was an expert on most materials, she knew Mary gave correct information to customers. She suspected that a lot of material was sold on the afternoons when Mary Wong worked.

It was ten before five when the bells above the front door rang their greeting. The older gentleman who entered had snow-white hair and a face wrinkled with years of smile lines. Despite his apparent age, he walked with a straight back and quick steps.

"Hello, Mr. Shelly." Mr. Shelly was the owner of Shelly's Cleaners and Laundromat. "How are you today?"

"Hello, Miss Monahan." Usually an optimistic person, he greeted her with little enthusiasm in his voice. "I've had better days, but there's no point in complaining."

Mibs noted that Mr. Shelly had several items of clothing in his arms. Each one had a numbered card pinned to it.

"Is there something I can do to make your day better?" she asked.

"I believe you can," Shelly replied. "The lady who does mending at my place of business sprained her wrist. It's a bad sprain, and the doctor said she can't use her wrist or hand for at least three weeks." With a hopeful expression, Mr. Shelly held the garments out in front of him. "Do you think you could take care of our sewing needs for the next few weeks?"

Reaching under the counter, Mibs pulled out an invoice pad and passed it to Mary. "This is Mary Wong. She does mending and alterations here at Monahan's." Mibs took the clothing from the older man and placed them on the counter in front of her employee.

Mr. Shelly nodded in relief and immediately stood in front of Mary. "How do you do, Ms. Wong."

Mibs gave her employee a supportive nod, and then she moved from behind the counter and out to the floor, where she began straightening various items in preparation for closing the store at 5:00 p.m.

After Mr. Shelly left the store, Mary carried the items in need of mending to the shop's back corner. Then, as she hooked the hangers on the rack, something fell and slid across the floor. Mibs watched Mary do a quick search, finding a metal key.

"Mibs," Mary called, "this key fell out of one of these outfits, but I'm not sure which one it came from."

Mibs accepted the key from Mary. Studying it for a moment, she said, "I don't believe it's a house key. I don't think it's a bank lock-box key. Hmm. Maybe it belongs to someone's gym locker." Handing the key back to Mary, Mibs made a suggestion. "Why don't we just mark it as coming from Shelly's and let them find the owner when they pick up their mending?"

"Sounds good."

"I'll lock the door if you will start counting the register," Mibs said. "While you close up the counter, I'll start sweeping the floor. Then we can both finish tidying up the materials."

The two young women finished the closing routine. Mibs turned the lock on the back door as Mary buttoned her jacket. Shadow gave a short bark and pushed her way past the two girls, positioning herself between her owner and the door. That meant that there was someone outside. The growl that had started coming from Shadow stopped. She began wagging her tail, indicating that the dog recognized the visitor approaching the other side of the door. Peeking out the door's small window, Mibs smiled. When she pulled the door open, they found a tall, dark-haired, brown-eyed man in the process of reaching for the doorbell.

Mibs waved. "Tony. I wasn't expecting you, but please come on in. It's getting colder out there."

With a quick goodbye, Mary Wong slipped out, and Anthony Vitali stepped in. Mibs watched until she saw her employee enter her car and start the engine before closing and relocking the door.

"Hi, Mirabelle." Tony was one of the few

people who frequently used her actual name. Or just as often used the nickname he'd given her when they were kids, *Wonderful.*

Slipping her arm through his, she escorted her childhood friend into the kitchenette between the storage room and the store's front. "I'll put some water on for hot tea."

"Put enough on for me, too," Aunt Bernie said as she came through the door that separated her rooms from the rest of the shop. "Hello, Anthony. How are you doing?"

Tony gave Bernie a gentle hug. "I'm doing good, Aunt Bernie." He guided her to the small table and chair set in the break area. "Let's sit down while the tea is being made."

While she waited for the tea to steep, Mibs texted Jace.

If you end up working late and don't get here for dinner, I'll put a container of sweet-and-sour barbequed pork in the little refrigerator. You can heat it up here or take it home.

The busy detective texted back an emoji of a smiley face.

When Mibs brought the tea tray to the table, she had added a dish of ginger-snap cookies for the three of them.

"Will Jace be coming by in a while?" Tony asked. Mibs had previously told him that Jace usually came by after work to pick up their shared dog, Shadow, and often had dinner with them. "I hoped to talk to him about something."

"I don't know. Jace is working on a new case, which is keeping him busy." Mibs studied her friend's thoughtful expression for a minute, wondering if she should ask him what was on his mind.

Suddenly, she remembered her important news, not believing she hadn't blurted it out as soon as Tony walked in the door. Mibs had called Aunt Bernie right after Jace confirmed the reservation at the church for their wedding. Tony and her best friend, Whitney, would be the next two she would tell.

"Tony, I want you to be one of the first to know that Jace and I have set a date for our wedding!" she exclaimed. "I hope you're free on February thirteenth."

"February thirteenth? I don't think I have anything scheduled," he replied. "If I do, I'll just have to cancel it. I'm not about to miss your wedding day." Accepting the cup of tea that Mibs handed him, Tony picked up the honey jar and squeezed a liberal dose into his drink. "Is there anything I can do to help with the preparations for the big day?"

"I'm sure there will be a lot you can do." She nodded. "In fact, I have a request that you might help with already."

"And what would that be?" Tony asked as he grabbed a cookie.

"When Jace called Father Smith to reserve the February date, Father asked that we sign up for six weeks of marriage preparation classes. We're supposed to meet Deacon Miller and his wife after eight o'clock Mass on Sunday. I know you often come to Christ the King Church when you're going to be tinkering with something at your 'fix-it' shop that day. If you plan to be in Havendale this Sunday, would you give Aunt Bernie a ride home after church?"

Tony gave Aunt Bernie a pleasant nod. "It would be my pleasure."

Mibs stirred in a spoonful of the locally harvested clover honey that she enjoyed in her hot tea. While she waited for her drink to cool slightly, she scrutinized the level-headed young man who sat across from her.

"Tony," she spoke softly, "would the something you want to talk to Jace about have anything to do with the research the two of you have been working on?"

He appeared to be carefully considering the question, shifting his gaze between Mibs and Aunt Bernie. Mibs suspected that Tony had agreed to review any information he came across with Jace before passing it on to Mibs in case it was something that would end up hurting her. Tony appeared to ignore the question. Instead, he asked, "Have you decided where you're going to have the reception for your wedding?"

Chapter 6

After Jace had walked Mibs to her car
following lunch that afternoon, he'd headed
back into the Gregory Tuppence Museum. He
pushed aside the thoughts about his upcoming
wedding and turned his mind to the ongoing
investigation. He'd learned how to
compartmentalize information and focus on the
job at hand.

Jace found Sergeant Brice Long and
Catherine Kind in the weapons room. Mrs.
Kind stood by the examining table, her hands
held together as if she was in prayer, her head
slowly moving from side to side.

"I can't tell you which dagger is the original
antique nor which is the copy," she declared.

"Who *would* know?"

Mrs. Kind turned when she heard the
question. "Oh, Detective Trueblood. You asked
who would know the difference. Mr. Patterson
would have probably been able to tell them
apart," she sighed, obviously dwelling on the
loss of the curator. Then, from the sudden
change in her expression and the widening of
her eyes, it seemed apparent that the woman
had just thought of something.

"You have an idea, Mrs. Kind?" Jace asked.

Peering up, she responded, "Yes. I remember
there was a voice message on the office phone
yesterday. Mr. Patterson had left for the
afternoon when I noticed a call from Dr. Jerome
Sassi. He's an appraisal expert for the

insurance company the museum uses, and he wanted to confirm an appointment with Roger Patterson on Thursday afternoon."

"Was this a scheduled visit, or do you think the curator called him for a specific reason?"

"We only call him when we have a new piece brought into the museum, a piece that Mr. Patterson felt needed to be examined for insurance purposes." The overwrought woman stared at the detective. "I don't know of any valuable items we've received recently or why the appraiser would be coming here this week."

Sergeant Long glanced at Jace. "Do you think he contacted the appraiser because he suspected that forgery and theft were happening?"

"That's a possibility," Jace said. "How is the inventory going?"

"It's more than half done. But, so far, we haven't found anything missing."

"After Mrs. Kind gets me Sassi's phone number, you two can finish. I have a feeling that if something is missing, it's been replaced by a duplicate."

Turning back to the manager, Jace asked, "Do you have a picture of the anelace that should have been in this sheath?"

"Yes, of course. We've photographed all the items in the museum's inventory."

Jace indicated the doorway with his open hand. "I'd like a copy of that picture, and I'd like to listen to the message you mentioned. Shall we go back to your office and do that now?"

Jace listened to the voice message, then directed Mrs. Kind back to Long. He then typed the appraiser's number into his cell phone. The call was answered on the second ring. After informing Jerome Sassi of Roger Patterson's untimely death, the antique and jewelry expert agreed to leave first thing the following day, hoping to reach Havendale by early afternoon.

Jace sat down in the wooden, hard-backed chair near the desk and leaned his head back. Running his hand through his thick, curly hair, he began sorting various pieces of information in his mind. Although there was still a lot to investigate about this crime, the possibility that Roger Patterson had intruded on a thief who was replacing valuable pieces of jewelry and other antiques with forged copies seemed a likely scenario. In doing so, the curator lost his life.

Once the appraiser got here, they could determine the extent of the thefts. One of the first things the lead detective needed to do was have a background check completed on each employee. *Did any of the workers at the museum have the skill to duplicate pieces so precisely? Would background reviews reveal any previous criminal activities? Or was the apparent forgery aspect just a red herring, and Patterson was killed for another reason?*

"Lieutenant..." Keil Harte interrupted his thoughts. "I believe we've found that missing short sword."

Jace followed Officer Harte to a storage dock in the museum's southern wing. Detective Mendoza was dusting a fourteen-inch knife for prints.

"What do we have, Juan?"

"There are no prints on the handle. It's wiped clean." Mendoza cut his eyes toward the lead detective. "But there are several on the blade."

Jace watched as Detective Mendoza carefully brushed off some of the chromatic powder he'd sprinkled on the smooth edge of the blade. Then, he lifted a print with tape and placed it on a fingerprint card. Repeating the process, Mendoza pulled off three more prints. "A couple of these prints are probably duplicates, but we'll get them sent to the lab."

"Any indication of blood on this weapon?" Jace asked.

"Don't know yet," Mendoza responded. "I'll have Officer Harte take it up to Benson to check for that."

Jace nodded. "Juan, I'll leave y'all to take over the investigation here. I'm going back to the station to go over whatever information Delgado might have found. Then, I'll order background checks on all the employees at this museum."

When he reached the front of the museum, Jace stopped to check in with Sergeant Long. "How's the inventory goin', Brice? Has Mrs. Kind found anything missing or out of place?"

Long folded his arms and shook his head. "Nope. Nothing seems to be missing, and we're at the end of the inventory list." He motioned toward the stress-worn manager. "I think she needs to get out of here, go somewhere, and recuperate."

"You're right," Jace acknowledged. "It was a lot to ask of her to get that inventory done today, but it was important." Jace's instinct told him that Mrs. Kind had found the deceased this morning just as she had reported, and she was innocent of any wrongdoing. But, just like everyone else connected to the museum, Jace would keep her on the suspect list.

He nodded at the museum manager. "Long, tell her… never mind. I'll tell her."

"Mrs. Kind," Jace addressed the woman, "thank you for your help today. I 'preciate you steppin' up to help with this investigation."

Trying her best to smile, Catherine Kind said, "If it helps catch whoever did this to Roger, it was worth the time."

"Yes, ma'am, that's true," Jace said. "Do you think you can get yourself home, or would you like me to have one of the officers take you? Sergeant Long could follow and drive your vehicle to your place."

Mrs. Kind assured him that she could drive. Jace accompanied her to a compact, two-door car.

Then he climbed into his truck and started the engine but didn't put it in gear. Instead, he leaned his head back, giving himself five minutes to catch a breath before heading back to Havendale Police Station.

~~

"You did a good job on these reports, Gene. You're getting better at doing interviews." He glanced at the young detective and smiled. "We'll make a detective out of you yet."

Since Delgado was younger and had fewer years as a detective than any others in the Havendale Detective Division, he was still called a rookie by some of the group. Jace knew he took the ribbing in good humor and wasn't surprised when he teased back.

"Yeah, boss, I guess a person has to be over the hill like you before they really know what they're doing."

Jace had asked Detective Clearwater to return to the station after notifying Roger Patterson's family. Eve had joined Delgado as he completed the interviews, helping him with the reports. Eve laughed at the verbal exchange. They all knew that joking was a way of lightening the tension that could build up during a murder case. Eve was eight years older than Jace, who had just turned thirty-three. She jokingly asked, "If Lieutenant Trueblood is 'over the hill,' what's that make me?"

"Umm..." Delgado opened and closed his mouth a couple times, obviously not sure how to answer the question without putting his foot in his mouth.

Jace piped up. "Detective Clearwater, that makes you a talented and dedicated detective who is an excellent addition to our team."

Gene Delgado cleared his throat. "That's exactly what I was going to say."

After glancing at the clock, Jace directed the two detectives to file their paperwork and head home. "I doubt if anything is going to change in this case before tomorrow. Try to get a decent meal and some rest. See you tomorrow."

Jace returned to his office and called Detective Mendoza. "Juan, how is it going? You guys about ready to stop for the day?"

"I was just sending everyone home. If anyone

else seemed in danger, I know you'd want us to work later. But, since that doesn't seem likely, I assumed we'd pick up the investigation in the morning."

"Good. I'll meet you here around 8:00 a.m., and we'll review everything then."

Chapter 7

Jace strolled up to Monahan's rear entrance and pulled out the key Mibs had given him. A black Dodge Challenger was in the parking lot: Anthony Vitali was visiting the Monahans. Before he inserted the key, he rang the doorbell and gave two knocks. That was the way Jace let Bernice and Mibs know it was him. As he pushed the door open, a friendly bark met him. Shadow padded up to his side and eagerly accepted the pats on her head.

"Hi, honey." Mibs greeted him, slipping her arm through his as they walked into the front of the shop. "I'm happy you made it in time to have dinner with us."

"Hello, Trueblood," Tony said, then turned his attention back to the plate of food in front of him.

"Hey, Vitali, did you leave anything for me to eat?"

"Only because I had to," Tony teased. "Mibs would smack my hand with a spoon if I tried to finish everything before you got here."

Jace kissed his girl on the cheek. "Good for you, sweetheart. Nice to know somebody's taking care of me."

He pulled out a chair and settled down next to Aunt Bernie at the large craft table that often doubled as a dining table. Jace sighed. "This smells good." He opened a Kaiser roll and placed it on the dish Mibs had put in front of him. He scooped a large helping of sweet-and-sour pulled pork onto the roll and reached for the nearby jar of pickles.

"I'll get you a salad bowl," Mibs said.

"Don't bother with that," Jace replied. Using salad tongs, he grabbed some of the lettuce and dumped it on his pulled pork, putting the bun top on and pressing the sandwich together. He didn't say anything else for the next few minutes except for 'Y*um*.'

"It would seem that you're hungry." Bernice smiled.

Jace nodded. Swallowing, he answered, "Guess I am, Aunt Bernie. If it weren't for y'all, I'd likely be gettin' fast food a little too often when I work late."

Bernie smiled fondly. "I'm happy having you join us for meals."

"Hey! What about me?" Tony gave a mock frown. "Don't I make you happy, too?"

Chuckling, Bernie said, "Anthony, except for the years you were away at college, I believe you spent more time with your feet under our table than at the one in your own house."

Tony raised his hands with the palms up as if to imply, 'what can I say?' He responded, "After my mom died, we had very simple meals. My dad didn't know how to cook much. So on the days I didn't follow Mibs home and have dinner with you two, Dad and I usually had hot dogs or microwaved mac-n-cheese." Tony gave the woman he'd adopted as a substitute grandmother a comically sad expression. "That means that you helped a young boy grow up healthy by providing nutritious meals several times a week."

Bernie chuckled again. "Oh, Anthony, you do make me happy."

As Jace listened to the reminiscences of times past that Tony shared with Mibs and her aunt, he felt a tinge of jealousy that he hadn't been there to join in making those memories. But that only lasted a few seconds. He realized that if he had grown up with Mibs, she might see him the way she now sees Tony. As a brother. And that was definitely not the way he wanted Mirabelle Monahan to think of him. Gazing across the table, he envisioned the life he and Mibs would share. With God's blessings, it would be a future where they would create memories with a new family of their own.

Jace finished his second sandwich and wiped his mouth.

Tony leaned back in his chair. "Mibs told me about the death of Roger Patterson. I knew him pretty well. There were several times when I ran across items that I believed were high-quality antiques at estate sales. So I took them over to get Roger's opinion and even donated an especially nice piece to the museum. He was a decent guy. I know you can't give us details about an active investigation, but is there anything you can tell us?"

"Not much to tell." Jace pushed his plate away and sat back. "We haven't gotten any reports from the lab yet, so I don't want to speculate." Jace added, "Sorry that you lost a friend. We will try our best to find the person who killed him."

"Thanks. I know you and your detectives will do a thorough investigation."

"Is that why you came by? To find out about Patterson's death?"

"No. I didn't even know about it until I stopped here, and Mirabelle told me." Tony glanced down for a moment before lifting his eyes back to Jace. "I came over to talk to you."

"Oh?" Jace started a question before he realized what Tony was hinting about. "Oh. Okay, maybe we should drive over to my house and have a chat."

Mibs interrupted before Tony could respond. "No. I don't think you need to leave. I wish you two would stop trying to protect me and just tell me what you've found out. Both Aunt Bernie and I know you guys are researching the lookalike girl in the pictures Whitney sent. I wasn't sure at first if I wanted to find out anything about who my father was or if there might be other relatives somewhere. After thinking about it, I realized that it would gnaw at me until I found answers." Mibs glanced at Aunt Bernie, who gave her a consenting nod. "We want to know what you two well-meaning men have found out."

"We just don't want you to get hurt." Tony offered her a sympathetic smile.

Jace placed his elbows on the table and rested his chin on his interlaced fingers. "Tell us what you've found, Tony. I imagine Mibs and Bernie will find out eventually. You know Mibs is like a dog with a bone when she gets it in her mind to figure out somethin'."

Tony reached into his back pocket and pulled out a piece of paper. He unfolded it and handed it to Jace. "That's a printout of the report I received today."

Hesitating, Tony rubbed his chin before talking. "Aunt Bernie, do you remember a few weeks ago when I asked if you had something that belonged to your deceased niece, Marian? After rummaging through your cedar chest, you found an old birthday card with an envelope Marian had sent to you and a bracelet once worn by her." He cleared his throat and took a sip of water before continuing. "I took them to a friend who works in a lab, and she was able to extract some DNA from both the envelope and the bracelet. I'd also swiped a glass, which Mibs had used. I gave that to her for comparison."

Mibs moved her chair closer to Aunt Bernie, taking the old, age-spotted hands and holding them gently with her own. The anxious girl asked, "Why would you do that, Tony? I thought you were searching for my father."

Tony turned to Jace. His furrowed brow seemed to convey a request for help in replying to Mibs' question.

Jace took a deep breath and let it out. "Soon after getting a copy of that picture from Whitney, I did a facial recognition search, and Tony did some internet research. We both came up with information that led us to a kidnapping that happened twenty-four years ago. Two little girls, identical twins, were snatched. One girl was returned safely to her parents, but the other was never found. The last place that one of the men suspected in the kidnapping was seen happened to be in the part of town populated by homeless people. This was the same area as St. Martin's, the shelter where Bernie picked up Marian Carpenter and her three-month-old baby."

A mixture of hurt and anger accentuated Mibs' words, "You're implying that my mother stole a baby. I can't believe that."

"No, I'm not saying that. From what your aunt has told me, Marian Carpenter would not have had the mental ability to participate in a kidnapping." Jace straightened and put his hands flat on the table as he regarded Mibs and Bernie. "Someone could have placed the child in her arms or left the baby where Marian would find her. If that had happened, I think her mind would've let her believe that it was the child she'd lost. Marian probably started caring for the baby as her own. So when she walked into St. Martin's, there wouldn't be any reason for anyone to think that the child wasn't hers."

"Aunt Bernie," Tony said, "I doubt if it even crossed your mind that there was a possibility your niece hadn't given birth to the baby."

Slowly shaking her head back and forth, shock and disbelief filled her face. "Marian had been gone for over a year, so I just assumed...." She placed her hand against Mibs' cheek. "I fell in love with that little girl as soon as my niece held her out to me, and I took her in my arms. Of course, it could be that my subconscious didn't let me consider such a thing. But realistically, I don't think my mind had been functioning fully because it was a difficult time. My brother Henry was dying, and I found myself at the age of sixty-three taking care of a less-than-functioning niece and a three-month-old baby."

"Wait, wait," Mibs exclaimed. "My mother being in Metrofield at the same time that a kidnapping happened could just be a coincidence!"

Tony pointed to the paper he'd handed to Jace. "I'm sorry, Mirabelle." He seemed to be forcing out the words. "The report is ninety-nine percent accurate. You and Marian Carpenter were not related. She was never your mother."

Mibs seemed momentarily stunned. Then, she slowly started shaking.

Jace shoved his chair back, and in a few quick strides, he was by Mibs' side. He pulled her into his arms and held her tight as the information seemed to slam through her. He wished he could take the shock and hurt from his beloved. Jace whispered in her ear, "It will be okay, sweetheart. It will all be okay."

As he comforted Mibs, Jace glanced at Bernice and saw her face visibly pale. He was glad to see Tony move closer to the stunned woman. "Aunt Bernie," Tony murmured as he reached for her soft, wrinkled hand, "are you all right?"

Patting the strong, slender fingers that held hers, Bernie nodded. "No matter what happens now, I'll still have the memories of all the joy and love I've had over the years with Mibs in my life." With a heavy sigh, she shook her head. "Anthony, I can't imagine what those parents went through when their babies were kidnapped. I remember when Mibs was four years old, and we were in a department store. I glanced down, and she wasn't by my side where she'd been ten seconds before. It took over five minutes to find her in the middle of a rack of dresses. She was just playing, enjoying the pretty colors and feel of the materials. But those were the longest five minutes of my life. What terror parents must feel when hours and days pass without finding a lost child."

Tony and Aunt Bernie turned toward the couple when they heard Mibs' shaky voice. "Who *am* I, Jace? Who *am* I?"

"If you mean who are your biological parents, we can do a DNA search and try to find out. But if you're asking who you...who Mibs Monahan is, I can tell you that." Jace tipped her chin up and gazed lovingly into her eyes. "You are the little girl that Bernice Monahan raised into a wonderful woman. You are the best friend that Anthony Vitali could ever have wanted. And you are the woman I love with my whole heart." He placed a kiss on the end of her nose. "That, my darlin', is who you are."

Mibs focused on Jace's face for several seconds before she kissed him soundly and then slipped out of his arms. She breathed deeply and slowly let the breath out. After repeating that action several times, Mibs squared her shoulders. Jace watched as the strong, determined spirit that he'd grown to know and love slowly made its way back into the mind and body of Mirabelle Monahan.

"If you and Tony think I may be the girl who got kidnapped from Metrofield all those years ago, then we need to find out." Cutting her eyes over to Tony and then back to Jace, she asked, "What do we do first?"

Jace ran his fingers through his hair. "I have the supplies in my truck to take a DNA sample. So why don't we start with that?" Reaching into his pocket, Jace pulled out the keys to his truck. "Catch, Vitali." He tossed the keys and watched Tony catch them. "There's a small crime scene kit, which I keep handy when working on a case. It's under the back seat. Would you get it, please?"

When Tony brought the kit in, Jace pulled out a DNA packet, labeled the swab envelope, and pulled out one of the two buccal swabs. Studying Mibs' expressive face to decide if she'd regained sufficient control of the roller coaster ride her emotions had to be going through, he asked, "Are you sure about this?"

She nodded.

He told Mibs to open her mouth wide, and he used the Q-tip swab to extract cells from inside her cheek, rubbing the swab up and down on the left side. He grabbed the second swab and repeated the process on the right side. Then, he sealed the samples into an envelope.

"I'm sure your lab friend could handle this sample." Jace glanced at Tony. "But I'm going to run it through CODIS, the Combined DNA Index System. We should find out soon if it matches anyone in the system."

Mibs stepped over to the end of the table, where Aunt Bernie had quietly watched the activity. Leaning down, she hugged the woman who had been her beloved caretaker since she was a baby and whispered, "I love you, Momma."

It was apparent that hearing that special endearment that Mibs had used only a few times over the years touched Bernie deeply. Bernie smiled, glancing up at the girl she'd adopted, now a grown woman. "I love you too, my dear. I always will."

Jace had closed up his forensics kit and reached for his jacket.

"Jace, would you take a walk with me?" Mibs asked.

He gave her one of his smiles, the kind that lit up his whole face. "I would love to go on a walk with you, sweetheart."

Hearing the word 'walk,' Shadow lifted her head, and her tail thumped the floor in eagerness.

Jace slapped his leg. "You know what the word 'walk' means, don't you, girl?" He chuckled. "Come on. You can come too." He turned to Tony. "Will you be here for a little while longer, Tony?" He didn't want to leave Aunt Bernie alone right then.

"Yep, for a bit longer. You go walk with your girl, and I'll stay here with mine." Tony smiled at Bernie. "What would you say if I stacked these dishes and then challenged you to a game of checkers?"

"I would say 'yes' to that idea, Anthony."

After Jace locked the forensic kit in the back of his truck, he took the leash from Mibs with one hand and reached for her arm with the other. "Are you okay?"

"No. Not really. Finding out who you thought

you were was a lie; the heritage and ancestors described to you as a child aren't really yours." The sun had already set, and moonlight shadowed Mibs' somber face. "I'm not okay, but...but I will be." She leaned her head against Jace's shoulder. "I believe the saying that God never gives us more than we can handle, but...."

"But sometimes the cross gets very heavy," Jace finished the sentence for her.

"Yes. It does."

As they walked, Jace tried to keep Mibs' mind off the upsetting information she'd just learned. "By the way, my mom called as I left the station. She asked if we had a set of china. If not, she wanted to know if you would be interested in the one she has."

"Aunt Bernie is giving us the set of Blue Willow dishes, which she inherited from her mother. I thought that we would use them most days."

"So, you don't need the set Mom offered?"

"That's not what I'm saying," Mibs responded. "Aunt Bernie always said her dishes were meant to be used. That's why we use the Blue Willow plates every day. But, it would be nice to have a set of good china for special occasions. What pattern is your mom's dishes?"

"Pattern?" Jace thought for a minute. "Well, they're blue and white with gold trim around the edge. I remember they have rows of ovals around some of the plates. I think Mom called them Wedgewood."

"Oh, the pieces of Wedgewood china I've seen were beautiful. I'm sure hers are lovely. Please tell your mom we'd love to have them. Maybe she could send a picture."

"Sure." Jace smiled at her response to his mother's offer. "Oh, yeah, she also said she'd like to have a wedding shower for us. Is that something you'd like?'

"Whitney is already planning to give us a shower. We should text Whitney your mom's phone number, so they can plan something together."

"Good." Jace pulled her a little closer as they strolled. "I didn't know there were all these extra little things connected to getting married."

"Hmm," Mibs murmured. "Talking about things for a wedding, we need to discuss our invitations. We can send a 'save-the-date' email out to those we want to invite, but I want to get actual invitations in the mail."

They reached the large gazebo in the town's small park. Jace unhooked Shadow's leash, allowing the dog to roll around in a patch of grass. Jace pulled a little orange ball from his jacket pocket and played fetch with their dog for a few minutes. After clicking the leash back on Shadow's collar, Jace put his arm around Mibs' shoulder, and the trio headed back to the shop.

Jace picked up the conversation as they retraced their steps. "Well, I guess ya better tell me what we need to do so those invitations get started on their way."

Chapter 8

When Jace reached the detectives' unit at the police station the following day, he found Juan Mendoza and Eve Clearwater already at their desks.

"Mornin', Eve. Starting early?" Jace asked.

"I'm researching the background of the two art handlers from the museum, Borne and Mosely. You said that you're hoping to find someone with the knowledge and skill to reproduce that dagger as well as other pieces of art. I thought they would be possibilities."

"Good," Jace responded. "Is Delgado planning on covering the research on some of them, or does he still have other paperwork to finish up?"

"We were able to finish the paperwork before we left last night. We'll split the names of the museum employees between us and let you know if anything seems promising."

"Thanks." Jace nodded at Detective Clearwater, then turned toward Mendoza. "Juan, would you come to my office?"

Detective Mendoza signed off his computer and grabbed a thick file from his desk. Sauntering over to the office, which displayed a new name placard by the door – *Lieutenant Jace Trueblood, Chief of Detectives* – he entered and slid the file across the desk to his boss.

"I'm still typing up a few notes from yesterday, but I figured you'd want to see what we have so far. We went through most of the museum, there are a few areas left to search, but I'd be surprised if we find anything else of importance." Juan plopped down in the chair facing Jace's desk.

Jace opened the file and started glancing through the information, stopping every couple of pages to read a few sentences.

"Toward the end, you'll find a note about a chair."

"A chair?" Jace lifted an eyebrow in curiosity.

Juan gave a slow nod. "One of the techs happened to notice a footprint on a chair in the entrance hallway. He only saw it while dusting for fingerprints near the front door frame. He leaned down, and the light hit at an angle that highlighted a slight indentation on the seat. When the tech studied it more closely, a faint shoe outline was visible. After taking analysis photographs, he covered the whole thing with plastic wrap and sent it to the lab. The lab specialists used an electrostatic dust lifter to pull the print."

"You know, Todd Benson had to use a short step ladder to reach the dagger hidden in that sheath."

"Yes, he did." Juan glanced at Jace. "Are we thinking the same thing?"

"Maybe the killer stood on the chair in place of a ladder?"

Juan nodded. "If we can get a good impression print, we might check shoes. What's that phrase Brice uses when we have a shoe imprint we're trying to match?"

"A Cinderella search." Jace grinned. "Let me know when we hear back from the lab.

Hopefully, we can get a good enough picture to obtain some search warrants. Try to keep this information quiet. We don't want our killer to hear about it and ditch his shoes."

"The chair may have been used that night. However, one of the employees could have stood on that chair for some other reason, at some other time."

Jace nodded. "Also, we're checking to see if an employee could reproduce that dagger. It might be that an employee worked *with* someone who has that kind of skill, and the employee was just the means to get into the museum.

"If that's the case, it will be harder to track them down." Juan sat forward. "Unless you want something else, I'll head back to the museum and finish up."

Subconsciously, Jace ran his fingers through his hair as he considered things. "Now that I think about it, I'd rather have Delgado finish up there. You fill him in on what's left to do. I'll have some of the team's analysts help Clearwater with the research instead of him."

"Okay. What do you want me to do after that?"

"After I finish going over this file, you'll come with me. I haven't had a chance to talk to Roger Patterson's wife and family. They're expecting me this morning." Jace reached for a bottle of water. After unscrewing the lid, he took a long swallow. "Detective Clearwater gave me her report after she notified Linda Patterson of her husband's death. Eve is pretty intuitive about judging people's reactions, and she didn't notice anything unexpected about the woman's behavior. Now that Mrs. Patterson has had a day to think about things, maybe something helpful has come to mind."

"We can get an impression on their reactions," Juan commented.

Jace nodded. "This afternoon, we should be heading back to the museum. The insurance company's appraiser, Jerome Sassi, is expected before three. I asked him to call when he gets close to Havendale. I'm anxious to see what he discovers."

Juan turned his head toward the door and listened. "I hear Gene Delgado's voice. I'll go fill him and Eve in on what you want while you finish reading the report."

Jace finished scanning the report, closed the file, and pushed his chair back. As Jace stood and moved around his desk, Captain Hank Taylor stepped into the doorway.

"Hello, Captain," Jace greeted. "Did you stop by for an update on the Patterson murder?"

"Good morning, Jace. I would like a report, but I stopped in for another reason."

As Taylor entered the office, Jace noticed a woman following behind him. In her late thirties, the woman was slightly built and had dark auburn hair and blue eyes. She stepped forward as the captain introduced her.

"Lieutenant Trueblood, I'd like you to meet Carla Hamman."

Jace offered his hand. "How do you do, Ms. Hamman?"

"It's nice to meet you, Lieutenant," she answered crisply.

The captain surprised Jace when he said, "I asked the clerk working right outside your door to move to another desk. Carla is going to take over that space."

"Ah...okay, Captain. Whatever you want." Jace waited for an explanation.

Smiling, Taylor said, "Carla is your new office assistant."

Jace lifted his eyebrows with that unexpected information. "I get an office assistant?"

"Yep. I told you that your new position would require extra paperwork. You've probably noticed that you get a lot more phone calls too. And I realized that your days are starting earlier and that you're staying here longer most evenings."

"That's true," Jace admitted.

"Carla has worked with me several times. She's very efficient; great with computers, paperwork, and maneuvering through red tape. If I hadn't inherited the assistant from the former captain, I would've requested her. Joshua, the person already in the position, knows all the ins and outs and is learning what I want. So, I recommended Carla to assist you."

Jace nodded as he considered the plus of having an assistant. "Ms. Hamman, welcome to the team."

"Thank you, Lieutenant Trueblood. Call me Carla; if you like," she replied.

"I think once Carla has learned what you need and what your preferences are, you'll find her an essential asset. After she's here awhile, Carla will know what should be brought to your attention and what you'd want to be handled by Sergeant Long." Captain Taylor added, "You'll be surprised how much of the paperwork she can handle for you, like forms and reports."

"That sounds great." Jace gave the woman an appreciative smile.

"One other thing, Lieutenant," Taylor said. "Could you have someone check into a break-in at Shelly's Cleaners? The report may or may not reach your desk since the patrolmen who answered the call listed it as vandalism. Shelly's is the dry cleaning service I use, and I happened to stop by this morning to drop off some things. Tom Shelly is convinced that it wasn't some juveniles causing vandalism. He showed me how bags were ripped open, several pants pockets turned inside out, and the desk area ransacked, but nothing was taken." The captain shrugged. "It may be nothing, but it won't hurt to double-check and put the man's mind at ease."

"We'll check into it," Jace assured him.

Glancing at the new assistant, Jace nodded. "Carla, do you think you can get settled in while I'm gone for a few hours today? If you haven't met Sergeant Long, I'd like you to talk to him. He knows just about everything that goes on in our division. And I'll try to set aside some time this afternoon for us to sit down and talk. If not today, definitely tomorrow morning."

Carla nodded. "I'll get my supplies moved into the desk and contact the IT department to have the phone system set, so it rings through my phone before routing to yours. I have met Sergeant Long; I'll ask him to fill me in when he has time."

Mendoza stepped into the doorway and stopped. "Sorry, sir. I'll come back."

"No, don't leave on my account. I'm done for now." Taylor peered at Jace. "Unless you have something major to report already, I'll follow up on the Patterson case later today. I have to be at a meeting in a few minutes."

"Thanks for the added help, Hank," Jace said as the captain headed for the door. Addressing the new assistant, he pointed to Juan. "Ms. Hamman, Carla, this is Detective Juan Mendoza."

Juan shook hands with her. "How do you do?"

"Hello, Detective Mendoza. Nice to meet you." As Carla left the office, she glanced back at her new boss. "I'll get settled."

"Do Clearwater and Delgado have the information they need?" Jace asked Mendoza.

"Yes. Delgado should be fine. He's going to meet some of Benson's crew at the museum. Eve's explaining what we want to the analyst and office personnel helping her."

Jace grabbed his jacket from a rack in the corner and motioned to the detective. "Let's head out, Juan. We're going to stop at Shelly's Dry Cleaning Service before we go over to talk to Mrs. Patterson."

After meeting with Tom Shelly and going over the break-in scene, Jace discussed the situation with Detective Mendoza. "Juan, I think Shelly may be right; it seems like someone had searched for a specific item. With the way the pockets were turned out, maybe something was left in a piece of clothing, which had been dropped off."

"Why not just wait until the dry cleaning was picked up?" Juan pondered.

"That is a good question." Jace clicked open the automatic locks on the truck doors, and they climbed into the crew cab. "I instructed Shelly to let us know if anyone acts suspicious or anything else happens that he thinks is important." Jace started the V-8 engine. "If there was something left in an outfit dropped there, either the owner needed it immediately, or a different person wanted it."

"Or the intruder decided to check pockets at random just to see if they found anything."

"I suppose that's possible." Jace put the truck in gear and headed for the small suburb on the west side of town.

When they reached the Patterson house, Linda Patterson provided some interesting information. She informed the detectives that she hadn't been able to think clearly when Detective Clearwater notified her of her husband's death. However, she seemed to be more focused today.

Mrs. Patterson escorted them into the living room, where she introduced her son and daughter-in-law. Detective Mendoza asked the younger Patterson couple to step into the kitchen, where they could talk.

"Please sit down, Lieutenant Trueblood," Linda Patterson said.

"Thank you, ma'am." Jace accepted the seat, a caramel-colored leather chair across from the matching couch Linda Patterson settled into.

"I'm glad you came over, Lieutenant. I don't know why I didn't mention it to the lady detective who talked to me."

"What's that, Mrs. Patterson? Did you think of somethin' you believe is important?" Jace noticed the shadows under the woman's eyes, indicating a poorly slept night.

"I don't know if it means anything, but my husband had been worried about a problem at work. He's stayed late several times within the last couple of weeks. Last week he went back to the museum during the night, well past 10:00 p.m. All he would say was that there was something he had to check out."

"Nothing about what he needed to check?" Jace tried to give his voice a relaxed and gentle tone, hoping to keep the recent widow calm and thinking clearly.

"I tried to press him on what worried him, but he wouldn't say any more."

"I'm assuming that he went back to the museum after it closed on Monday night."

"He apparently did, but I didn't realize that until the next morning. I'd developed a migraine and had taken medicine. When I finally fell asleep, I slept deeply and woke up later than usual. I just thought he'd left for work early that morning."

When they left the Patterson home, Juan informed Jace that neither Luke Patterson nor his wife had much to tell them. Luke had told Juan that he could tell something had been bothering his dad, but Roger Patterson wouldn't talk about it."

"Well, I think we were probably correct in thinking he suspected someone of stealing antiques from the museum and leaving forged replacements." Jace checked the road before pulling away from the curb. "Juan, I'd offer to buy you lunch, but I want to stop by and see Mibs for a few minutes. Mind if I drop you at the station?"

"No problem. I'll get something to eat, then check on Delgado and see if he found anything of importance."

Chapter 9

As Jace opened the door of Monahan's Sewing Shop, two ladies stepped out. Holding the door for them, he nodded. "Good aft'noon, ladies."

Smiling, one of the women replied, "Thank you. Good afternoon to you, too."

Inside, Jace was greeted with a cheery, "Hello, Detective Trueblood."

"How are you, Mrs. Maxwell." Jace's stepped up to the counter. "Unless I'm on official business, why don't you call me Jace?"

"Okay, Jace. As long as you call me Deanna."

"Sounds good," he agreed. Jace glanced around the room.

"Mibs is in the office with Bernie. They're sending in their supply order."

He stepped around the counter, where he found Shadow waiting for a greeting. Jace patted the dog on the head and headed to the tiny office. Stopping in the doorway of the small room, he observed the two ladies, Bernice sitting on a chair behind the desk and Mibs standing over a computer as she typed in information.

"That should do it, Aunt Bernie. I think we ordered everything we need." As Mibs turned her head to address her aunt, her face lit up when she saw Jace standing there. "Hi, honey."

"Hi, girls. Thought I'd stop by and see how you two are doing." Jace gave them a warm smile. "Have you eaten lunch yet?"

"No, we haven't," Bernice said.

Mibs exited the webpage she'd been using to order from Sims Wholesale Sewing Supplies. Walking behind the desk chair, she offered Aunt Bernie her arm to aid the aged woman in standing. Mibs handed a cane to her aunt as they stepped toward the entrance.

Jace moved back. "I'm glad you haven't had lunch because I ordered pizza. It should be here any minute."

"Mmm, pizza." Mibs reached for his hand. "What kind did you order?"

"I know you like the veggie pizza, so I ordered a large. Hope you don't mind; I had the pizza place add sausage."

"Sounds yummy. Is that okay with you, Aunt Bernie?" Mibs asked.

"Yes. Sausage and vegetables sound good."

"I'll check with Deanna and see if things are fine at the counter." Mibs headed to the front of the shop.

A few minutes later, the trio sat at the small break table, reaching for pieces of the hot, cheesy pie. Jace studied the faces of the two women sharing lunch with him. He noticed Bernie's unusual quietness and couldn't detect the sparkle that normally shone from Mibs' eyes. Jace worried about the effect the DNA test results might have had on each of them. The information Tony gave them the night before had hit both women hard.

"Bernie." Jace studied the dear, old aunt. "How are you holding up?"

Sighing before she lifted her eyes, Bernice replied, "I'll be all right. Sometimes it just takes a little time to absorb unexpected information."

Jace was used to seeing this indomitable lady face challenges head-on, finding the best solution for each situation. But this dark cloud obviously hung heavy on her mind and in her heart. Turning to Mibs, Jace reached over and ran his hand down her face. When her troubled green eyes focused on him, he asked softly, "Mibs, what about you? Is there anything I can say or do?"

She gave a half-hearted smile and shrugged. "What's there to do? It is what it is. I guess we'll just wait and see if my DNA matches the girl who disappeared twenty-four years ago."

Taking her hand in his, Jace mumbled, "I wish Whitney had never seen that other girl. I wish she'd never sent that picture. We shouldn't have started searching."

"No, Jace..." Mibs stopped him. "Maybe it's better to know now. What if this happened later, maybe years from now? If we found out after we had half-grown children, how would it affect them?" Mibs shook her head with determination. "We need to find out the truth, then let life settle into some kind of normal."

Jace lovingly studied her face. "Sweetheart, I think in a lot of ways you're stronger than I am."

"I think we're stronger together." Mibs gave him a decisive nod.

Bernie cleared her throat. "I think you both should eat your pizza before it gets cold." Picking up her glass of tea and slowly swishing the ice around, she asked, "Have you found out who killed Roger Patterson?"

Jace shook his head as he placed more pizza on his plate. "We've sent several things to the crime lab but don't have the results back yet. I'm meeting an appraiser for the museum this afternoon. We hope he might shed some light on the case."

"How is Catherine Kind doing? I heard she is the one who found the body," Bernie asked. "I've known her since before the museum opened. In fact, about four years ago, Catherine asked me to do a bit of work for the museum."

"I didn't know that." Mibs' mouth fell open.

"It was after you started college. Catherine had a tablecloth, well over a hundred years old, she wanted to use for a display. However, it needed repairs on the lace edging, and she couldn't find anyone else in the area who knew how to do tatting. So I finally agreed to tackle the job with the understanding I would do it at my own pace. I knew my fingers would stiffen up if I worked more than half an hour at a time."

"So..." Jace tilted his head. "What is tatting? I'm trying to understand some of the sewing terms, so I can follow the conversation when Mibs tells me about her day."

"Tatting is a way of making lace formed by a pattern of rings and chains. You use a tatting shuttle and create a lot of double stitches and picots. It depends on the design you want," Bernie explained.

Jace still didn't understand. Rings and picots?

"Mibs or I can show you sometime," Bernie told him.

Deanna interrupted the group. "There is a guy out front who wants to know if we can order upholstery material."

"I'll go talk to him, Mibs. You stay and visit with Jace." Bernie grabbed her cane and used the edge of the table to pull herself up.

Mibs pushed her plate away and leaned back in her chair. "Besides working on the Patterson case and worrying about me and Aunt Bernie, do you have anything else happening?"

"Well, Juan and I checked out a break-in at Shelly's Cleaners and Laundromat." Jace reached for the last piece of pizza, stopping for a second to ask, "Did you have all the pizza you wanted?"

"Yes, please finish it."

"Anyway, the patrol officers think it was kids causing mischief. Tom Shelly believes whoever broke in had been searching for something. I'm leaning toward his way of thinking. I just have no idea what they would have been searching for." Grabbing the pitcher of tea, he refilled his glass. "I sent a tech over to lift prints, but since so many customers come in, I think it's unlikely we can isolate a specific person's prints as being relevant."

"We're doing some mending for Mr. Shelly. He's such a friendly and upbeat person. I hope he doesn't have any more trouble."

A phone chimed, and both Mibs and Jace reached for their cell phone. It took only a second to realize it was the police-issued phone in Jace's pocket. After answering the call and talking for a few minutes, he pushed back his chair.

"I have to go. Dr. Sassi, the appraiser, will be at the museum shortly. I want to be there to meet him." He drained his drink and transferred his last piece of pizza from his plate to a napkin. Jace picked it up to take with him. Placing a kiss on Mibs' cheek, he murmured, '*I love you*' in her ear and headed for the door.

~~

It was only after Jace left that Mibs remembered the key that had fallen out of Shelly's clothing. Could that have any connection to the break-in at the dry cleaners?

When Mibs entered the front of the shop, she saw Aunt Bernie at the cash register checking out a customer and Deanna helping a couple near the muslin and batting display. The bells above the door chimed as a middle-aged man entered. Mibs forgot about Shelly's key when the man handed her a list of sewing items, which his wife had asked him to pick up.

"No problem," Mibs assured him. "Let's start with the snaps and thread, then move down the list."

After Mibs had assisted the helpful husband in completing the shopping list, she escorted him to the counter. There, waiting with a wide grin on his face, was a man in a pale blue bib-front western-style shirt embellished with large brass buttons. He held his gray, flat-brimmed hat in his hand. Tucked under one arm appeared to be new blue jeans.

"Hello, Mr. Buckmore," Mibs greeted the local private investigator.

"Miss Monahan," his bellowing voice reverberated across the room. "Got some more jeans for you to shorten for me. I'd really like them done this week. Do you have time?"

"I'll make time for you, Mr. Buckmore."

Many people in Havendale found Macey Buckmore loud and annoying. But Mibs had developed a soft spot for the PI after he'd provided a photograph that depicted a man named James Hornsby and his co-conspirator, Wendy Black, during a previous murder investigation conducted by the HPD. A surge of sadness floated through Mibs' mind as she remembered the deaths of Jasmine and Jennifer and the investigation that followed. The picture Macey had taken added a second motive to why Hornsby would kill his kind, gentle wife, Jasmine. The first time Mibs met Jace had been during the investigation of those murders. Now, Mibs accepted Buckmore's booming voice and less-than-genteel manner as part of his personality.

"Same length as always? Or do you want to try them on, so we can mark the length?"

"They're the same brand I usually get, so go with the usual length." Macey plopped the three pairs of pants on the counter. Reaching for Mibs' hand, he gave it a tight squeeze and a vigorous shake. "Thanks. Call when you have them ready, and I'll surely come right over."

As soon as he left, Mibs shook her hand and moved her shoulder a few times to counteract the over-enthusiastic handshake.

Mibs heard a soft chuckle. Turning to face the counter, she saw Mary Wong, who had just signed in for the afternoon shift. Mary covered her mouth with her hands, trying to hide her amusement at the last customer's actions.

Mary peeked up shyly. "A person certainly knows when Mr. Buckmore is in the room."

"Yes, they certainly do," Mibs agreed as she continued to rub her arm. A few seconds later, both girls were laughing out loud.

Still smiling, Mibs handed the jeans to Mary. "I know you have a few other mending items to complete, but try to fit these in, too. Let me know when they're done, and I'll call our friend, Mr. Buckmore."

As she walked away from the counter, Mibs realized that despite the downhearted feeling that had gripped her since the previous night, she was still able to laugh. What was that old saying? *Laughter is the best medicine.*

Mibs went back to work on the second Renaissance-era costumes ordered by the Havendale Community Theater. She'd finished the first one last week and had made good progress on the second. Mibs scrutinized the outfit on the dressmaking dummy. She inspected the laced bodice and flared bell sleeves, lifting one of the sleeves to check the armband insets. By the end of the day, she should be able to call Mrs. Barns to schedule a fitting. Mibs clipped the pin-filled cushion to her wrist and then knelt down to adjust the dress's hem.

She ignored the phone when it rang, knowing that Mary would answer. Mibs looked up when Mary walked over to tell her about the call.

"Mr. Shelly asked if we'd found anything in

the bundle of mending he'd left with us," Mary said. "I let him know that a key had fallen out of one of the outfits. Then, Mr. Shelly explained how a guy came for his cleaning and became agitated when he was told that a pair of his slacks had been sent to Monahan's Sewing Shop to be mended. The guy asked if anything had been found in his clothing. Mr. Shelly told him no, but he may have missed something before he sent them to be mended."

Mibs thought about the break-in at the cleaners. The key that had fallen from the items to be mended came to mind. *That certainly wouldn't have been what they wanted, would it?* If someone needed that key, they would have just returned to the cleaners and asked for it, like that customer had done. *Wouldn't they have?*

~~

Hours later, just past midnight, Bernie and Mibs were both suddenly awakened by a blaring blast from an alarm. Mibs grabbed her cell phone and hit the speed dial button for Aunt Bernie's number.

The phone was quickly answered. "Mibs, are you all right?" Bernie shouted against the background noise of the alarm.

"I am, Aunt Bernie, are you?"

By the time her aunt assured her that she was okay, Mibs had already reached the bottom of the steps and headed toward Bernie's room. As she passed into her aunt's bedroom, shut and locked the door behind her, the cell phone rang.

"Mibs?" Jace's concerned voice reached her ears. "I just got a call from the alarm company.

I'm on their call list. Is everything okay?"

"Aunt Bernie and I are fine. I came straight to her room and locked the door. I haven't checked anything else."

"Stay where you are. The alarm company has already called the police; a patrol car should be there any minute. I won't be far behind."

Mibs had climbed on the bed with Bernie and put her arm around her aunt's shoulders. Several minutes passed before she heard Jace's voice.

"Mibs, Bernie?" Jace knocked on the bedroom door. "You can unlock the door now."

As soon as she opened the door, Jace gently grabbed her shoulders and held Mibs at arm's length, running his eyes over her to ensure she was okay. Then, glancing past her, he asked, "Bernie, are you okay?"

Bernie nodded. "Yes, I am. Why did the alarm go off?"

"The patrolmen are still checking, but it appears that someone tried to force open the window in the corner of the stock room. I'd say they used a crowbar or something similar." Jace put his arm around Mibs. "There isn't anyone around now."

"I'm glad that you and Tony installed that alarm system. It really makes a loud noise." Mibs rested her head on Jace's shoulder.

"Do you think someone tried to get to the cash register?" Bernie asked, leaning back against her solid walnut headboard. "Don't think anyone would break in for material or patterns."

"That's probably the likely reason." Jace

nodded. "Anyone with much sense would figure that most businesses put their cash away in a safe at night, not leave it in the register."

"Well, people with common sense aren't the ones who usually try to break into buildings," Mibs concluded.

"What is it?" Mibs asked when she noticed a thoughtful expression on Jace's face.

"I just thought about how this is the second break-in within a couple days. Maybe we do have some vandals in the area. I might add another car to the night crew for a while."

Bernie said she would try to go back to sleep, snuggling back against her pillows.

"Would you like some tea?" Mibs asked Jace after they'd reached the small galley kitchen.

"No, thanks," he replied. "I'm going to step out and check with the officers outside."

Returning a few minutes later, Jace told Mibs that the patrol car would cruise by every so often and keep an eye out for intruders. "It's not likely anyone will return tonight, but I can sleep on the couch in the break area if you'd like."

"No. There's no reason for you to stay. Besides, you have to work in the morning." Mibs gazed into his eyes. "Go home and get some rest."

"Yes, ma'am." Jace smiled before he kissed her goodbye. "I'll reset the alarm on my way out. Good night, darlin'."

Chapter 10

Jace returned to his house on Maple Street and accepted Shadow's greeting as he entered the front door. The two of them trudged back upstairs. Shadow curled up on the dog bed and quickly settled down. Jace tossed and turned as his mind kept him from relaxing. He wouldn't be able to force himself to fall asleep, so he laced his fingers together and put his hands behind his head as he began thinking about the information uncovered by Dr. Jerome Sassi.

Sassi held several degrees, including gemology, curatorship, and business. It hadn't taken long for Jace to appreciate the appraiser's talent as he carefully made his way through the pieces of antique jewelry. Within the first two hours, Sassi discovered a fake diamond and emerald bracelet. The bracelet in the case was not the same bracelet appraised when the museum first opened, a good replication, but a fake.

Jace called to mind what Sassi had said about another forged item found in the display. "This is the piece that Roger Patterson called me about." He'd held up a beautiful ruby necklace. "Patterson was right about it being a forgery." Sassi had signaled Jace to come over, putting the piece back under a jeweler's scope. The specialist had moved the fake aside and picked up a ruby pendant, explaining what differences to search for. "This one is real."

They had stayed at the museum until after

9:00 p.m. before Jace suggested the appraiser stop for the night and head to a local bed and breakfast. Jace and Juan headed to their homes with a plan to meet at the station before joining Sassi back at the museum at 10:00 a.m. the next day. Jace had swung by to pick up Shadow on the way to his house and was sound asleep when the alarm company called.

After mulling over the day's events for almost an hour, he finally drifted off, waking to the buzzing of the alarm at seven the next morning.

He walked into the office at 7:45 a.m., finding Carla Hamman working diligently at her desk.

She glanced up over the top of her glasses. "Hello, Lieutenant Trueblood."

"Hello, Carla. Give me a few minutes to organize things, then maybe you can come in, and we'll have that chat we never got around to yesterday."

"Yes, sir," Carla replied. "I made some fresh coffee. Would you like some? I hear you like your coffee black."

Jace stopped and turned to face the new assistant. "I wouldn't mind a cup, but I don't consider git'n' coffee one of your jobs."

"I wouldn't have offered if I thought you expected me to wait on you." Carla gave him a teasing smile. "Captain Taylor and I used to take turns grabbing the drinks; I just thought I'd see if you wanted to do the same."

"Sure. Sounds good to me." Jace grinned. "Better tell me how you like your coffee, so I get it right when it's my turn."

"Actually, I don't drink coffee. I prefer root beer or water."

"Root beer or water, got it." Jace gave a nod and then headed for his office.

Carla stepped through the open door fifteen minutes later. She held a coffee in one hand and a notepad lying flat in the other. Two napkins with pastries and a water bottle were moored on top of the pad. Setting the coffee and then the tablet down on Jace's desk, Carla offered, "Lieutenant, would you like a cherry Danish or a bagel with cream cheese?"

Jace's mouth turned up in a half-grin when she didn't wait for an answer, placing the Danish beside his coffee and the bagel next to her notepad. "I like Danish. Thank you," he said.

By the time the next hour had passed, Jace and the new assistant had developed a cooperative work relationship. Jace could tell that Carla Hamman would make his new position as a lieutenant a lot easier as far as paperwork went. He watched as she took careful notes of what he thought were priorities and what items could be put on the bottom of the list. Jace appreciated that she nodded when he asked her to rearrange some of the files.

Jace slid a paper across the desk. "This is a printout of my team's requested days off for next month. Would you have time to go over it and see that there aren't more than one or two people requesting the same days?"

"I can do that." Carla picked up the form and slid it into the back of her notepad.

"That reminds me." Jace sat up straight. "I

better put in my request for February. I'll be in big trouble if I don't."

"Vacation?" Carla queried.

He smiled widely. "Honeymoon." Reaching for the picture on the edge of his desk, Jace turned it around. "This is my fiancée, Mibs."

Carla focused on the photo and gave an approving nod. "Congratulations, she's a pretty young lady." Carla turned to a new page and wrote in large letters. *Must have - time off.* She peered up at her new boss. "Well? What are the dates? From when to when?"

"Ah...I'm taking two days off before the wedding and the week after. That would be... February the 11th through the 21st. Coming back on the 22nd." Raising a brow, he asked, "Are you gonna file the request for me?"

"Yes, I will."

"Thank you. I'd 'preciate that."

After knocking, Detective Clearwater stepped into the office, waiting until Jace acknowledged her presence.

"Detective Clearwater, come in." He gestured toward Carla. "Have you met the newest member of our team?"

"I have," Eve responded. "Sergeant Long introduced her to everyone in the office yesterday." She lifted her hand in greeting. "How's it going, Carla?"

"Good, so far. I think I'm going to like working in this unit." Carla stood up. "Lieutenant, is there anything else you need at this time?"

Jace shook his head. "We went over a lot of things already. Hope I didn't overwhelm you."

"No problems. I'll get started on my list."

"Thanks.   And would you please send in Detectives Mendoza and Delgado?"

"Yes, sir."

Jace pointed to the chair. "Eve, what have we got?"

"I have the information on the Tuppence Museum employees." Paging through a set of papers she'd brought with her, she pulled out several printouts. "I've marked three of the workers as possibly having the ability to forge jewelry or antiques."

"Three?" Jace was surprised that three people would have that ability at one museum.

"I'm saying it's possible, not necessarily probable. I'm basing it solely on the suspect's school and work history."

Detectives Juan Mendoza and Gene Delgado entered the office. Mendoza leaned against the wall near Jace's desk. Delgado scooted the second chair forward and sat down.

"Eve was just telling me about employees from the museum." Jace nodded toward Detective Clearwater. "Go ahead with what you were about to say, Eve."

"Before Joe Craton retired and took the job as a security guard at the Gregory Tuppence Museum, he worked at Bossley's Jewelry Store for many years. He was an expert at cleaning and repairing jewelry. He also handled special orders and was well-known for making one-of-a-kind engagement rings. Apparently, he took the job as a guard because he wanted to keep busy; he found retirement too boring."

"Wasn't it Craton's sweater that had the

bloody handkerchief in the pocket?" Delgado asked.

"It was," Jace answered. "But it seems odd that he'd take time to hide the dagger used for the stabbing, then leave an incriminating piece of evidence like a bloody handkerchief where the police could easily find it." He shrugged. "But if a person is nervous and in a hurry to get away, they might not be thinking clearly."

Eve moved to the information on the next employee. "There are two art handlers who both have degrees in art history. They unpack, inspect and catalog new items in the museum and anything else required to care for the antiques. Nick Mosely has been working at the museum for six years. Other than that one degree, he doesn't have any other expertise. Mosely started at Tuppence right after he graduated from college. If what Mosely said in the interview is true, Roger Patterson taught him his job's requirements. I doubt he could forge antiques or jewelry." Detective Clearwater tapped the top of the next paper. "Albert Borne, on the other hand, helped pay his way through college by working at a jewelry restoration business that specialized in repairing and restoring antique and vintage jewelry. He also had a part-time job in the university's history and archeology department."

"Borne sounds like someone we should definitely check out more closely," Mendoza said.

"There's one more," Eve added. "Patrick Clyde is a part-time postgraduate student who only works on Fridays and Saturdays at the museum. He already has a master's degree in art, and now he's working on his doctorate, hoping for a career as a curator in a top museum. He plans on getting a Ph.D. and is currently researching ancient weaponry."

"Ancient weaponry, such as antique Toledo steel daggers? Hmm." Jace sat forward and drummed his fingers on his desk. "We have three possible suspects if we don't count Mosely, and that's not considering the possibility that an employee might be working with someone unknown to us."

"Where do you want us to start, boss?" Detective Delgado asked.

Jace pushed back his chair and stood. "Right now, Juan and I need to get back to the museum and meet with Dr. Sassi. Gene, you and Eve start delving a bit deeper into these three employees and double-check their whereabouts at the time of Patterson's death. Have one of our analysts check out the financials for each of these people. See if there are any unexplained large deposits within the last couple of years." Jace pulled on his coat. "Let's try to meet back here between 3:00 and 4:00 to compare notes."

Chapter 11

Jerome Sassi had stopped at the Havendale Police crime lab before returning to the Gregory Tuppence Museum. Jace had asked the appraiser to study the two seven-inch knives at the lab and let the crime scene technicians know which dagger was authentic. After carefully scrutinizing both blades, Dr. Sassi had no trouble pointing out the genuine antique. He was now working with the detectives as they combed through the rest of the museum's treasures.

"This diamond and sapphire broach is not real." Sassi slowly shook his head. "Take a peek through this scope, Detective Trueblood." The expert beckoned Jace with his hand. "Do you see that tiny bubble on the very edge of this sapphire? A real stone would not have that." After letting the detective study the indicated gem, Sassi picked up the broach and held it up. "A genuine blue sapphire would be deeper in color and would not reflect the color like this when moved in the light. Also, it's easy for me to see that these are not real diamonds."

~~

It was another long day, past 7:00 p.m., before the detectives and appraiser left the museum. Jace called Mibs and let her know he'd be late picking up Shadow. He insisted that Dr. Sassi and Juan let him buy them dinner. Jace had been willing to pay for a meal at a nice restaurant, but Jerome Sassi surprised him when he said that a hamburger and fries sounded good to him.

As they ate their dinner, they discussed Sassi's findings.

"Four pieces of jewelry and the antique silver and gold dagger. I would imagine the total value of all those items would be pretty high." Jace dipped a French fry into tangy ketchup.

"My goodness, yes," Dr. Sassi confirmed. "We're talking several hundreds of thousands of dollars. That ruby necklace alone is valued at over ninety thousand dollars."

"Wow!" Delgado exclaimed. "Somebody has been making themselves rich. I wonder how long they have been exchanging these reproductions at the museum."

"Unless there's more than one person, a team of forgers perhaps, then I'd say the thefts have been going on for a couple years." Sassi took another bite from the quarter-pound cheeseburger. After swallowing, he added, "It would take some time to reproduce pieces that were good enough to pass casual inspection—not something done in a couple days."

"If we find any unexplained large deposits in one of the suspects' finances, it might lead us in the right direction." Jace caught the eye of the waiter and signaled for the check. "You've been a real help, Dr. Sassi."

Sassi frowned as he regarded the detective. "Lieutenant Trueblood, do you think the stolen items may be recovered?"

Glancing up, Jace considered the question. "Maybe. If we catch the assailant, we might find where he hocked the jewelry pieces. Depending on where and who they were sold to, there is a possibility of finding them." He shrugged. "But they may be long gone by now, with no way to trace them."

Sassi sighed and shook his head. "I hope the stolen items are located. I hate to report back to my company with the huge claims these losses will bring."

It was after 9:00 p.m. when Jace dropped Dr. Sassi off, then drove over to Monahan's Sewing Shop. As expected, when he pulled into the lot, the downstairs was dark. Aunt Bernie would be settled down for the night. The upstairs light shining from Mibs' small efficiency apartment wouldn't be on much longer. When Jace quietly unlocked the back entrance and opened the door, he found Shadow waiting. Letting her slip outside, he stepped in long enough to reset the alarm, then relocked the door. The duo climbed into his truck and headed back to Maple Street. When Jace pulled up to his home, his dad's truck was in the driveway. The porch light and the inside hall light were on, but the rest of the house was dark. From the text he'd received that morning, Jace knew the aged-but-experienced carpenters had arrived and started remodeling the downstairs bedroom. Surmising that Dad and Uncle Jack had retired for the night, he entered the house, tiptoeing to avoid waking them.

Because of the alarm company's previous night's interruption, Jace went straight to bed and quickly fell into a deep sleep. He awoke easily in the morning, ready to start the day.

After having a quick breakfast with his dad and uncle, who assured him they were fine making the planned updates to the bathroom without him, he headed to work.

~~

"Good morning, Lieutenant," Carla greeted Jace. "We have some reports from the lab. I set them on your desk."

Jace placed a bottle of water and a can of root beer on her desk. "Thank you, Carla. I hoped to hear from them."

"The coffee should be done if you want to help yourself." Carla smiled when she noticed the cold drinks. "Check your email. The response for your requested days off should be in your inbox."

After reading through the lab reports, Jace phoned Captain Taylor's office. The call was answered by his assistant, Joshua.

"Is he in yet?" Jace queried.

"Not yet, Lieutenant, but he should be here soon."

"Please ask him to call me when he gets in."

"I will," Joshua began, then stopped. "Hold on. He's walking in now."

A moment later, Jace heard the captain's voice. "What's up, Jace?"

"Hank, based on lab reports we got back and information we've obtained from the insurance specialist's appraisal on items at the museum, I'd like to request search warrants on several suspects."

The captain didn't take long to consider the request. "Bring what you have down to my office, and let's go over everything."

Once in the captain's office, Jace spent several minutes bringing Captain Taylor up to speed on the information the team had collected during the last couple of days. Handing the report from the lab to the captain, Jace pointed out relevant items. "We've established that the forged dagger was the murder weapon. With the insurance company's appraiser's help, we now know that at least four jewelry pieces have been replaced by reproductions. So I think we'll be able to narrow down our list of suspects by using a shoe print we found."

"A shoe print?" Taylor's eyebrows peaked. "Is this print from the murderer?"

"We're fairly sure it is," Jace stated. "When the lab tested the imprint found on a chair at the museum, they extracted small traces of blood where the shoe's heel would have been. The blood belonged to Roger Patterson."

Jace explained their belief that the killer had used the chair to reach the long knife's sheath to hide the dagger. If they could match a shoe to the imprint they have, they would almost assuredly find the person who stabbed the curator.

Captain Taylor reached for the phone. "Give me the suspects' names, and I'll see how fast I can get you those warrants."

Detective Clearwater left her desk and met Jace at his office door as he returned from his conference with the captain. "Lieutenant, one of our computer specialists just gave me the financial information on our subjects. I think you'll find one particularly interesting."

"Well, well," Jace murmured as he studied the paper. "I see deposits corresponding to his weekly paycheck, but I wonder where these other large deposits came from."

"Should we bring him in?" Eve asked.

"Let's wait. I'm hoping to have search warrants soon. As soon as they arrive, I want Borne, Mosely, and Clyde called back to the station."

"Not Craton or Jackson?" Eve questioned. "And what about the women?"

Jace shook his head. "According to the crime lab, the imprint of the shoe is a men's size eleven. I've seen both women, and neither has a foot that large. Also, Joe Craton is a small man; I'd say his shoe size is a nine, maybe nine and a half." Jace tapped the report showing the financial information. "I think we know who will match the imprint we found, but I don't want to tip him off by calling only him. We'll head to his house and search if he isn't wearing the shoe to match our sample when he gets here. We'll also search the other suspects' houses. We need to cover all possibilities."

Chapter 12

"Mibs." Mary Wong walked into the back area. "I finished all the mending. Would you like me to call the customers and tell them their things are ready to be picked up?"

"Thank you, Mary. That would be good." Mibs ran the box cutter over the seam of a large cardboard box and pulled open the container holding bags of polyester stuffing. "If you do the others, I'll call Macey Buckmore. I have something I want to talk to him about anyway." She closed the box cutter and slipped it into her pocket. "Mary, where did you put that key that came from the items brought in by Tom Shelly?"

"I put it in a small bag and taped it to the invoice." Mary gave her employer a questioning glance.

"I'm curious if I can figure out what that key might open."

Mibs headed to the counter and pulled out the invoice for Shelly's Cleaners and Laundromat. Removing the key, she took a blank piece of paper and placed it over the key. Then, using the tip of a pencil, she ran it back and forth over the key, creating an exact impression. She then placed it on an empty spot of the paper and traced the outside. On the outlined sketch, she added the number etched on the key, 57.

Macey Buckmore didn't answer when she called, so she left a voicemail. A short time later, he called her back. "Miss Monahan, I got your call." The man's voice came through clear and loud, even over the phone. "I'm calling you back like you requested. Do you have my jeans ready?"

"Hello, Mr. Buckmore. Your jeans are ready to be picked up." Mibs cleared her throat. "I wanted to make sure I was here when you came to the store. I have a question to ask you when you arrive."

"Okey-dokey. How about right away? I'm free now."

"That would be good. I'll see you soon." After ending the call, Mibs stood at the counter, staring without seeing as her thoughts wandered around in her mind. Her attention came back into focus when the front door opened.

"Tegan!" she exclaimed. "I planned on calling you and the others as soon as I got a chance." Mibs occasionally had lunch with a few of her friends from high school. Tegan, Olivia, and Sophie would often meet Mibs to spend an hour or so visiting.

Tegan placed a garment bag on the counter and grinned. "I got your email. I already marked the date for your wedding on my calendar." The young woman began bouncing on her feet with excitement. "Valentine's weekend – how exciting and how romantic! What can we do? Is there anything we can help with? We should have a shower."

"My friend, Whitney, is planning a wedding shower. I gave her your names, so all three of you should be getting an invitation soon." Mibs thought for a moment. "Actually, if you, Sophie, and Olivia really want to help, I hope you might be willing to take charge of the decorations. I know we have almost ten weeks, but that isn't a lot of time to get everything done."

"Oh, yes, yes." Tegan nodded. "I'd be glad to, and I think Olivia and Sophie would too. I'll call them as soon as I get home." Clasping her hands together and leaning forward, she asked, "What color theme do you want?"

"Well." Mibs tilted her head as she considered. "I've always liked blue-green shades like teal or turquoise. But since it's going to be Valentine's Day weekend, I wonder if I should use red and white."

"You can still go with a blue-green color; if you want, use red to add a contrasting color. Like—maybe have red and white roses with teal ribbon."

After considering the idea, Mibs nodded. "The bridesmaids could wear teal dresses and carry white flowers with a few red mixed in for contrast. That would be nice. Wouldn't it?"

Tegan nodded. "I like that idea. Maybe I can find streamers with hearts on them."

"Whatever the three of you think would be good. I'll trust your judgment. I can give you money before you start or just keep the receipts. Then I'll reimburse you."

"Just tell us where the reception will be, and we'll handle the decorations."

"Jace and I reserved the community hall at our church. I'll text you the contact information. Now, back to business." Mibs pointed at the garment bag. "Do you need some alterations?"

Tegan unzipped the bag and pulled out a pleated mid-length skirt with a wide, fitted waistband. "I need this skirt shortened about two inches. I wasn't sure if I could do a good job with all the pleats. Would you be willing to tackle it?"

Mibs nodded. "We can handle this. I see you have safety pins marking where you want the hem."

"Yes."

After her friend left, Mibs hung up the skirt and headed back to the box of polyester stuffing. When she reached the shelving unit, she found Mary sliding the last bag of stuffing onto the shelf. "Mary, you are worth every penny I pay you!"

The young woman blushed. "Thank you. I try to do a good job."

The bells above the front door jingled, announcing the arrival of another customer. Leaving Mary to break down the now empty box, Mibs headed toward the front. Before she reached the counter, a robust voice rang out.

"Hello. Anybody home?"

"Hi, Mr. Buckmore," Mibs greeted him. "Thank you for coming right over."

"No problem." He scanned the store. "Are you holding down the fort by yourself today?"

"My helper, Mary, is here. Aunt Bernie's friend took her to a doctor's appointment this afternoon." Mibs stepped a few feet away from the counter and called, "Mary, could you keep an eye out for customers for a few minutes?" As soon as her employee responded, she turned back to the private investigator.

"Mr. Buckmore, would you come back to my office for a bit, so we can have a conversation?" Mibs reached under the counter and pulled out the paper with the tracing.

"Sure thing," he quickly responded.

When they stepped into the office, Mibs gestured toward one of the two chairs in the small room. After the PI sat down, Mibs leaned against the desk. "Mr. Buckmore," she began.

"Hey, Miss Monahan," he interrupted. "How 'bout you just call me Macey?"

"Okay...Macey," she said. "Then, please, call me Mibs." She cleared her throat and tried again. "Macey, I'd like to offer you a trade. I'll trade the sewing job the shop just did on your jeans for a little of your time as a private investigator if you're willing."

"Oh? A little barter, huh?" Tapping his booted foot on the floor, Macey nodded. "What do you have in mind?"

Handing him the paper, Mibs asked, "Do you know what this key would open?"

After studying the picture for a moment, Macey sat back. "I have a pretty good idea. I'd say it's from one of the lockers at the bus station."

"The bus station?" Mibs repeated in a questioning tone.

"Yep. I've used those lockers myself, so I recognize the key." Then, sitting forward, he questioned the seamstress. "You want me to find out what's in that locker? Can you let me know what I'm searching for?"

"Actually, Mr. Buck…, ah, Macey, I'm not sure what we're trying to find. But I believe this key might be what someone is trying to find. I believe the same someone who broke into Shelly's Dry Cleaners tried to break into here." Mibs proceeded to tell the private investigator about the break-ins that were currently being blamed on vandals. She also explained her feeling that the key was a clue to something more than vandalism.

"I see what you're getting at." Macey twirled his cowboy hat around in his hand as he thought about the situation. "How 'bout I do a little snooping and see if anybody is using that bus station locker?"

"That would be good, Macey. However, I don't want anyone to get upset with you if they find you hanging around for too long."

Macey chuckled. "Don't worry about me. I'm a master at blending into different places and situations."

Mibs squinted at the exuberant investigator. She tried to imagine the colorful man with the round face, large belly, and recognizable western attire effortlessly blending in anywhere. "Okay, I'm sure you know how to do your job."

As Mr. Buckmore left the building, he held the door for Aunt Bernie and Marge to enter. Her aunt clutched a bag from the local pharmacy.

"How did the check-up go, Aunt Bernie?" Mibs scanned her aunt's face, hoping she'd gotten a good report.

"Pretty well," Bernie said before giving a slight shrug. "The doctor changed my blood pressure medicine. He's worried because my blood pressure's gone up again. What's he expect? I'm eighty-seven. I think I'm in pretty good shape for my age."

Mibs bit her lip to keep from letting her worry show. She wanted to take care of her great-aunt, just as Bernie had cared for her through the years. "Would you like me to make you a cup of tea?"

"No, thank you, Mibs. Marge and I met Hazel at the café, and we had tea and cakes." Aunt Bernie leaned on her cane and made her way around the counter and to her room. Marge followed closely behind. "I'm going to lend Marge a couple of my Perry Como and Nat King Cole albums."

Despite the worry about her increasing high blood pressure, Mibs was glad to see her beloved aunt enjoying time with her friends.

Mibs smiled when she heard Mary's comment.

"I hope I'm still going out to have tea and cakes with my friends when I'm her age."

Chapter 13

A rap on the door frame made Jace glance up from the paperwork, which had been absorbing his attention. Jace set his pencil down and waved to Sergeant Long to enter. "Brice, what do you need?"

"I want to let you know that you have company." Stepping forward, Brice jerked his head toward the bullpen outside the lieutenant's office. "I asked them to wait by my desk, so I could give you a heads-up before sending them back."

"That sounds ominous." Jace sat back as he studied the desk sergeant. "What kind of visitors do I have who would compel you to give me a warnin'?"

Brice gestured with an open palm. "At least one of them is an FBI agent. They said it was a personal matter."

"Hmm. I have no idea...." Jace stopped halfway through his response. Calling to mind the DNA request he'd sent through CODIS, he suddenly realized why the FBI might be stopping by. He peered at his friend and colleague. "Brice, do you know anything about Mibs Monahan's parents?"

Shrugging, Brice answered, "Only that they died when she was young, and she was raised by her great aunt."

"I suspect this visit may have to do with the DNA search I'm doing, trying to find out if Mibs has any other relatives."

"Why would the FBI be interested?"

Jace frowned. "I know you and Juan are friends with Mibs and Bernice Monahan besides being my friends." Hesitating, he studied Brice before he continued. "I'll tell you the whole story later, but for now, I'll just tell you that there's a question as to the real identity of Mibs' parents."

Brice narrowed his eyes. "Say that again."

"Hold on a minute, Brice. I haven't had time to check all my emails this mornin'." Tapping a few keys, Jace waited for the emails to load. Opening the one from CODIS, he read through the information. Sighing loudly, he let the information sink into his mind. Mibs' DNA matched a baby who had been kidnapped twenty-four years ago. Clara Richmond.

Jace glanced at his friend. "Send them back. And Brice, maybe you and Juan could come in here and hang out in the background. I want you two to hear this too."

Sergeant Long nodded without any added comment, turned, and headed back to get the two men.

Jace stood as two men entered his office. A tall, middle-aged man in a dark suit, white shirt, well-polished shoes, and carrying an overcoat across his arm stepped up to the desk. A slightly younger, blond-haired man followed close behind. He was wearing khaki pants and a polo shirt under a dark peacoat.

The taller man held out his identification. "Detective Lieutenant Trueblood, I'm special agent Ted Dasher." Motioning toward the other man, he added, "This is Mark Gage."

Jace carefully studied the ID, noting that the agent was part of the FDDU, Federal DNA Database Unit. "Hello, Special Agent Dasher." Glancing at Mark Gage, he asked, "Are you with the FBI also, Mr. Gage?"

"No." the man stepped up. "I'm a private detective. I work out of Metrofield. One of my clients is Jackson Richmond, and I'm here representing him and his wife, Crystal."

Jace slowly nodded and studied the two men. "Pull up a chair, gentlemen."

As Dasher and Gage sat down, Detective Mendoza and Sergeant Long quietly stepped into the room and lingered near the back wall. Mark Gage didn't seem to notice, but Special Agent Dasher did. Dasher ran his eyes over the uniformed sergeant and the dark-eyed man wearing a dress shirt, tie, and sharply creased slacks. After giving them the once-over, he turned back toward the lieutenant.

Focusing on Jace, Dasher asked, "Lieutenant Trueblood, you ran a DNA match request through CODIS. I'd like to know where you got the DNA sample and why you checked it."

Cutting his eyes over to Mark Gage, Jace said, "I suppose you are here for the same reason."

"Of course I am," Gage responded. "This concerns a case that my father started working on over twenty years ago. When I took over his private detective business, I promised that I'd continue checking on this case at least once a year." Gage leaned forward, determination etched on his face. "Since we'd checked for updates year after year, the FBI gave us a call when there was a hit on this particular DNA."

"Gage." Agent Dasher got the PI's attention and gave him a cautioning stare. "Let me ask some questions."

"Lieutenant," the FBI agent squinted at Jace, "would you like to tell us what you found?"

Jace reached for the picture resting on the side of his desk. Turning it around and sliding it forward, he answered, "I'm checking for her. She wants to know where she came from."

Gage leaned forward, then suddenly grabbed the picture. "This looks like Camilla."

Jace picked up his phone and pulled up a picture that had been forwarded from Mibs' friend, Whitney. "This, I've been told, is Camilla Richmond. The picture was taken last summer at some charity function in Metrofield." He pointed to the picture of Mibs that the private investigator still held. "That's a young woman named Mirabelle Monahan who lives here in Havendale."

"May I see?" Dasher asked. Scanning both images, he nodded. "They could be twins." Without taking his eyes from the pictures of the lookalike girls, he asked, "If you know this is Camilla Richmond, you might know what happened to her and her sister twenty-four years ago."

"A friend and I have been doing some research, and we found information from a cold case about a kidnapping that happened in Metrofield."

Dasher handed the phone and the framed photo back to Jace. He then reached into his pocket and pulled out a small notepad similar to the one Jace always carried. Opening the pad and turning a few pages, he read a name, "Anthony Vitali. Would that be your friend?"

Raising his eyebrows, Jace nodded. "I hope Tony hasn't been delving into places on the internet where he shouldn't. He's been a good friend to Miss Monahan since they were kids. He just wants to help."

The FBI agent frowned. "He came pretty close to crossing the line; he really straddled the fence a few times. But not so much that I'd be able to make a case against him." Sitting back, he chuckled. "Actually, if I hadn't been assigned this case after your request came in and was specifically watching for things connected to it, I doubt his online inquires would have even been noticed. He definitely knows his way around the net."

"So… Monahan, did you say?" Dasher pulled a pen from his pocket. "How do you spell her name?"

"M-i-r-a-b-e-l-l-e M-o-n-a-h-a-n."

Dasher wrote in his notebook as Jace spelled the name. "She goes by the nickname of Mibs." Jace leaned his arms on the desk and stared at the agent. "And she's the woman I'm engaged to marry."

"So this woman who exactly resembles Camilla Richmond is your fiancée?" Special Agent Dasher stared at Jace. "How did you get this picture from the event in Metrofield, and what made Miss Monahan start asking questions?"

Juan and Brice's enquiring expressions made Jace pause. He knew they must be wondering about this DNA search and the kidnapping.

Jace held up the phone with the photo and motioned with a tilt of his head. Juan stepped up and accepted it. Then, moving back to the other side of the room, he shared the picture with Brice.

Jace spent the next ten minutes giving Dasher and Gage an abbreviated version of how Mirabelle Monahan was raised in Havendale. Brice and Juan listened to the information, too.

Mark Gage shook his head in bewilderment. "You're telling us that back when the kidnapping occurred, little Clara Richmond was left somewhere by one of the criminals? A homeless woman found the baby and claimed it as her own? Somehow this woman ended up back here in Havendale with the baby? Are you serious?"

Ignoring Gage's questions and tone, Jace gave his attention to Dasher. "Agent Dasher, can you tell me where the FBI believed the second kidnapper was last seen with the Richmond child?"

"From the reports I've read, they lost track of the suspect in the downtown area where a large number of homeless people were known to congregate." He rubbed his chin as he considered the possibilities. "You said that this woman, Marian Carpenter, had lost touch with reality when her husband and daughter died in a fire. Her family would have to often search for her when she started roaming the streets trying to find her dead family?"

Jace nodded. "From what Bernice Monahan knew and from what she was told by the sister at St. Martin's homeless shelter, the scenario of how Mibs ended up here in Havendale made sense. All these years, Mibs has believed that she was the daughter of Marian Carpenter."

"What a minute," Mark Gage interrupted. "I remember reading in my father's file that he talked to a sister when he made the rounds of the homeless shelters." Gage opened a large manila folder and thumbed through a pile of papers. "Here it is. He talked to Sister Theresa at St. Martin's shelter and soup kitchen. She didn't know anything about the baby."

"St. Martin's?" Jace slowly nodded. "That's the name of the homeless shelter where Bernice Monahan picked up her niece, Marian, and the baby." Jace tried to remember the exact words Bernie had used when she gave him the information. "I think your father talked to the wrong sister. I'm sure Bernie said that the sister who called her and met her when she drove to St. Martin's was named Sister Mary Rose. Maybe the sister who was interviewed by your father didn't know about the baby."

"So," Dasher said, "the nun from the homeless shelter contacted the Monahans to let them know where the missing Marian Carpenter was staying. Her aunt, Bernice, drove to Metrofield and picked up Carpenter and the baby." Shaking his head, he asked, "Why did they automatically believe the child was hers?"

"Why not?" Jace questioned. "Marian Carpenter had been missing for over a year. She said it was her baby. Why would they think it wasn't?"

"Tell me, Trueblood, why now? Why, after all

these years, did Miss Monahan decide that Marian Carpenter hadn't been her real mother?"

"It wasn't something that Mibs decided. It was basically tossed into her lap. We weren't even thinking about Mibs not being part of the Monahan family when we started this research. She'd never known who her father was, so when her friend, Whitney, started seeing a woman who resembled Mibs so closely, the question about possible relatives came up. That's what got this DNA thing started."

Standing, Mark Gage closed the manilla envelope. "Where is Miss Monahan? I want to interview her."

"Hold your horses," Jace cautioned. "I'm not going to let y'all barge in and start questioning Mibs. When Tony brought a report from the lab and told her that Marian Carpenter had never been her mother, it *hurt* her. It was like someone had left her floating in the middle of the ocean without a life raft. I'll go talk to Mibs first, then call you when you can see her."

"Now, just a minute," Gage argued. "This case has been on the books of Gage Private Investigations for over two decades. If this woman is the missing Richmond daughter, I don't want to waste more time. I can find her where she lives without your help." He turned and addressed Agent Dasher, "Are you coming?"

The FBI agent watched Mendoza and Long quietly move to block the doorway. Flicking his eyes toward Gage, Dasher sat back and folded his arms. "I don't think we're going anywhere for a bit."

Jace and Dasher locked eyes. Even though Jace didn't say anything about his men's actions, he was sure the FBI agent saw the fleeting smile that crossed his face.

"Wouldn't do any good for you to head over to Monahan's right now," Sergeant Brice said in his calm, slow voice. "There'll be a safety check going on by the time you leave here. You'd just end up sitting in your car while waiting to get through the check site."

"We'll go around," Gage insisted.

Juan shook his head, "Nah. Wouldn't help. This is a small town. No matter which way you go, you'd still have to go through the safety site to reach your destination."

Dasher glanced back at the two police officers, then looked at Jace. He'd obviously decided not to try and call their bluff. He sat patiently. Dasher had been an agent long enough to know it was better to go along instead of bucking a stacked deck.

Jace lifted his arms and stretched. Then he pushed his chair back, stood, and grabbed his coat. "I'll ask my assistant to get you some coffee while you wait."

"Are you going to let them get away with this?" Gage asked the agent.

"Sit down, Gage," the agent said. Then, as Jace slipped on his coat, Dasher requested, "I'd like double cream in my coffee, please." Tilting his head toward Gage, he added, "When we stopped to get gas on the way to Havendale, he added a sweetener to his coffee."

Jace gave a quick nod and headed out the office door. Brice remained standing against the wall while Juan walked around to the far side of the desk and took over Jace's chair. The detectives, the agent, and the PI began to talk as they waited. Detective Mendoza told them about the young woman known as Mibs Monahan. He gave them a good picture of her strong spirit and kind heart. He talked about Bernice, the great-aunt who had devoted the winter of her life to caring for and guiding the little girl who had become her adopted daughter.

~~

Thirty-five minutes later, Juan's phone rang. He listened, then hung up and gave the two waiting men the address of Monahan's Shop.

Chapter 14

After leaving the police station, Jace drove to Monahan's Sewing Shop and parked in the lot behind the store. He unlocked the back entrance without ringing the bell and let himself into the storeroom. Walking toward the front, he stopped when he noticed the open office door. "Hi, sweetheart."

Mibs' face lit up with pleasure when she saw him in the doorway. "Hi, honey. It's a nice surprise to see you at this time of day." She moved away from the desk, meeting him halfway as he entered the small room. She slipped her arms around his neck. Jace pulled her close and bestowed a lingering kiss on her lips. When he finally pulled away, her eyes shone.

"Darlin', I try so hard to protect you, to not let you get hurt." Jace frowned. "I'm not doing a very good job."

"What is it, Jace? What's...oh,...you got the results from the DNA, didn't you?"

Jace took a step back, and taking both her hands in his, he told Mibs about the test results.

Mibs let go of his hands and paced back and forth a few times before she responded. "So I am the missing girl. I'm Clara Richmond from Metrofield." She bit her lip and stared at Jace. Then she took a deep breath. "Do you think my biological parents will want to meet me? Do you think they even think about me after all these years?"

"Sweetheart, I'm sure they will want to meet you. They never stopped searching for you."

"Really? How do you know?"

Jace described the FBI agent and the PI waiting at the police station. He explained how the Richmond family had kept Gage Investigations on retainer for the past twenty-four years. And how a call was made each year to check on any possible information. "I didn't want them to come here until you and Bernie had a chance to prepare yourselves."

Mibs squared her shoulders. "Call them. Tell them to come over. I'll go talk to Aunt Bernie."

~~

Mibs informed Deanna that she and Bernie would be in the break area for a bit, and she should call out if needed. Mibs sat on the sofa, talking to Aunt Bernie while Jace made tea. When the jingle from the front doorbells echoed through the shop, Jace was the one who went to the front and escorted the two men to the back.

Jace introduced FBI Special Agent Ted Dasher and PI Mark Gage as they walked into the break area.

Mibs stood up and faced them.

Mark Gage stopped and stared. "I can't believe how much you resemble Camilla," he stammered.

Agent Dasher stepped around the shocked PI and presented his identification to her. "How do you do, Miss Monahan. I'm Special Agent Ted Dasher." He observed the white-haired lady studiously watching from the plaid-cover sofa and nodded. "You must be Bernice Monahan."

"I am," Aunt Bernie answered. "Please sit down." She pointed to the chairs around the small break table. The two men turned chairs to face the couch, then sat down. Shadow paced the floor between them and the sofa several times before lying down on the floor in front of Bernie. The dog's eyes locked on the two men, ears flicking each time Dasher or Gage made any movement.

"I'm assuming that Lieutenant Trueblood told you that we showed up at his office because his submission of your DNA to the CODIS system rang some bells and sent out notifications in our system."

Mibs nodded as she took a seat next to Aunt Bernie. "When I discovered that Marian Carpenter was not my biological mother, I decided to find out who I was, who my parents were." She focused on the agent, then turned to the investigator. "Are you sure that I am the girl who went missing all those years ago?" Taking a deep breath, Mibs asked, "Do you believe I'm Clara Richmond?"

Gage seemed reluctant to answer for a moment. After studying the girl's green eyes, light red hair, facial features, height, and build, he slowly nodded. "I believe you are. You are the first one of all candidates who showed up over the years that I truly believe may be Jackson and Crystal Richmond's daughter."

"What do you mean all the candidates who showed up?"

"There have been quite a few girls over the

past twenty years who claimed to be the lost child."

"Why? Why would someone claim to be who they weren't?"

Gage gave a short, mocking cough. "For the reward, of course. For the chance to be taken in by a rich and influential family."

Mibs' eyes widened. Her disbelief was replaced by surprise, then hurt, then anger. "Tell Mr. and Mrs. Richmond that I want to know the truth. But I don't need their money. I have a good life and people who love me. I'm happy being who I am." She drilled Mr. Gage with a steely stare. "I don't want anyone implying otherwise."

Shadow sensed the tension in the air and growled lowly, eyes laser-focused on the man who seemed to be upsetting Mibs.

Mibs reached down and gave Shadow a comforting pat.

Gage shook his head. "I'm not implying that of you. I merely said that there had been those who have done so in the past. So you can understand why I've developed a healthy skepticism over the years."

"Miss Monahan," Agent Dasher interrupted. "It is simple enough to prove the identity of your biological parents. The DNA test that your fiancé ran is proof enough for me. However, to alleviate any doubt on the part of others, I'd like to have another test done using a blood sample. We can send it to Metrofield and let Jackson Richmond have a doctor or lab that he trusts perform a second DNA test."

Mibs sat quietly, casting her eyes down.

Aunt Bernie picked up her hand and held it gently. Mibs gazed up at her aunt, who gave her a reassuring smile.

Mibs finally turned toward the agent. "I will do the test, so there will be no doubt." She straightened. "Is there anything else you need or want to ask?"

Dasher directed his question to Aunt Bernie. "I don't suppose, after all this time, you would know what the baby was wearing when your niece brought her to the shelter. They never described the clothing that the two girls were wearing. The FBI, at the time, thought it would be helpful to not release a couple things, to help weed out false calls."

Aunt Bernie squeezed Mibs' hand tighter. "Were the kidnapped girls wearing pink rompers and matching booties?"

Dasher and Gage exchanged looks for several beats. Turning to Aunt Bernie, Dasher asked, "Is a romper a one-piece outfit?"

Bernie nodded, "That's usually what it is referring to." She turned toward Jace. "Would you give me a hand, please? I want to get something out of my cedar chest where I store keepsakes."

Without hesitation, Jace offered Bernie his arm as she pulled herself up and leaned on her cane. He then followed as the old aunt slowly walked to her bedroom.

"I think I know what she's getting," Mibs said to the two astonished men sitting on the hard-backed wooden chairs.

~~

When the notice that a hit had been

confirmed on Clara Richmond's DNA, bringing up a cold case from years ago, Ted Dasher was prepared for the worst. After all this time, he imagined that the DNA request was because a small, long-deceased body had been found. If not that, then they would likely be encountering a person of nefarious character who'd kept the girl all these years. When he found Miss Mirabelle Monahan and Bernice Monahan, her white-haired elderly aunt, he didn't see any reason to bring down the full force of the FBI. While waiting in Lieutenant Trueblood's office, Dasher started checking the information the detective had given him by using his phone to send requests to the home office. A few minutes ago, he'd received a response to those inquiries, an email confirming the deaths of Marian Carpenter's husband and child. The office had also found validation that the Havendale police had been enlisted to search for the wandering Mrs. Carpenter on several occasions. So far, the story had checked out. When he finally accepted the possibility that the Richmond child had been raised by a caring woman because of a misunderstanding, the FBI agent adjusted his plan of action. He hoped there would be a way to reunite the family without causing unnecessary pain to any of those involved.

Dasher smiled when Bernice returned a few minutes later, holding a clear bag.

"I was given this when I retrieved my niece and the baby from St. Martin's Homeless Shelter. Sister Mary Rose said that the little girl wore it when Marian showed up the day before." Smiling at Mibs, she said, "I kept it because it's what I'd put on you when you were baptized."

Gage held his hand out and took the clear bag in which the romper and booties had been stored. Then, placing the pieces of baby's clothing on the table, he slipped a picture out of an envelope and put it beside the baby's outfit. They matched. All the skepticism that had plagued the long-time investigator was gone. Pulling his phone out, he walked to the other side of the room. "I have to call Mr. Richmond."

"Miss Monahan," Agent Dasher said. "I doubt if we need that second blood test."

"Yes, we need to have the extra DNA test run. I don't want there to be any doubt. Not for them and not for us," Mibs announced emphatically.

"Excuse me, Mibs." Deanna walked in. "I have a sewing emergency, and I'm not sure how to handle it."

"Do you want me to see what it is, my dear?" asked her aunt.

"No, thank you, Aunt Bernie. I think I need to step away and think. Having a distraction for a few minutes might help."

Agent Dasher focused on the perceptive hazel eyes of Bernice Monahan. "Ms. Monahan, while your niece is taking care of her customer, perhaps you can give us a detailed description of the day you brought home Clara...ah...the little girl you thought was your niece."

~~

Mibs greeted the customer who waited at the

counter. "Hello, what can I do to help you?"

A frazzled woman wearing a light aqua, two-piece suit with a mandarin collar jacket gazed hopefully at the seamstress. The lady appeared to be dressed for a special occasion. "My daughter, Katie, is making her Confirmation this afternoon. She accidentally caught her dress on the corner of a shelf, and it tore. There's no time to go shopping for a replacement. Please, can you repair it?"

Mibs carefully ran her eyes over the beautiful princess-style dress made from a delicate floral embroidered lace fabric. She tapped her finger against her chin as she studied the approximate five-inch tear on the lower side of the dress's skirt. "I believe I can help save this dress. Deanna, would you go to the notions wall and get me a package of ultra-light *Stitch Witchery* tape, please?"

As her employee grabbed the requested item, Mibs headed back to the corner where an ironing board was set up. She plugged in the iron and carefully set the desired temperature. Mibs used a measuring tape to ascertain the tear's exact length plus a quarter inch. Having used the fusible tape before, Mibs knew that she needed a similar piece of material to bond the torn area together for this delicate fabric. She cut a narrow strip of material from a bolt of sheer lace. She measured and cut the needed piece of the bonding material and placed it between one edge of the tear and the thin strip of lace she'd cut from the bolt. Mibs placed a pressing cloth on top. She judged that she used enough but not too much heat for the delicate fabric, then she let the fusible strip of adhesive melt, creating a bond between the fabric pieces. She completed the repair by repeating the process for the other edge of the tear.

Mibs held the dress out to Katie's mother. "I don't think the repair will be very noticeable. Please, see what you think."

The anxious woman accepted the dress and scanned the skirt, searching for the mended area. "Where..." she pondered. "Where did you fix it?" When she held the dress up to the light, she found the spot she hunted for. "Oh, here it is." She gave Mibs a grateful smile. "The repair isn't even noticeable unless you make an effort to search. Thank you. Thank you so much." The happy patron opened her purse. "How much do I owe you?"

Mibs waved the question away. "No charge today. A young person's Confirmation Day is a special time. Consider my few minutes of work a gift."

After escorting the woman to the door, Mibs thought about how the almost hidden repair she'd made with the fusible bonding reminded her of the term she'd mentioned to Jace, *stitch in the ditch* – another way to hide something in plain sight, in that case, a seam of thread. Those thoughts reminded her that Jace was still working on a murder case, a case he was most assuredly anxious to get back to. Instead, he was here with her and Aunt Bernie, ready to give them any kind of support they might need.

Mibs returned to the break area, approached Jace, and kissed him on the cheek. "I know you need to get back to the police station. Go on. We'll be fine."

~~

"Are you sure?" Jace studied the tilt of her head and the determination in her eyes. He nodded. "Okay, I do have to get back to work. Promise you'll call if you need anything?"

"I will. Now, go."

As he headed for the back door, he stopped and gave Dasher and Gage his business card. "If anything new comes up, or if you need any information, call *me*. Do you understand?"

"I don't...." Gage started saying.

Special Agent Dasher spoke over the investigator's words. "We got it, Lieutenant Trueblood."

~~

After Jace left, Mibs focused on the FBI agent. "Agent Dasher, please take the blood sample. Then, Aunt Bernie and I have a business to run."

"Wait," Gage demanded. "Miss Monahan, Jackson Richmond wants you to come to Metrofield. He even said he'd send his jet to pick you up."

"No," Mibs responded softly. "I very much want to meet Mr. and Mrs. Richmond."

Mibs had been too young to remember Marian Carpenter, the woman who she'd always believed was her mother. She had no memories of any parent other than Aunt Bernie. Unexpectedly learning that she did indeed have parents had been a shock. The idea of getting to know a new family had thoughts floating through her mind to the point that her head ached. How would this new revelation change the life she knew?

"But until they absolutely, positively have no doubt in their minds about my identity, I'll stay here at my sewing shop."

Chapter 15

After the agent and private detective left, Aunt Bernie went to her room, and Mibs joined Deanna in the shop. When the door opened shortly before 4:00 p.m., Mibs greeted the man who entered, then stopped to study him a second time. He was not too tall but had a round middle and a round face. The gray coveralls and black hair momentarily confused Mibs.

"Macey?"

"Didn't recognize me at first. Did you?" Buckmore chuckled enthusiastically. "I told you; I know how to go incognito."

"You are definitely full of surprises," Mibs conceded. As long as he didn't speak, he could go unrecognized. But, on the other hand, it was unlikely that he could disguise his not-too-soft voice. "Please come in. Let's go to my office."

The private investigator took up most of the tiny office they stepped into. Encouraging Macey to sit on the wooden chair, Mibs leaned against the desk.

"I sure do have some information for you, Missy," Buckmore announced. "It's surprising how people ignore maintenance and cleaning people. When a guy at the train station stepped up to locker 57, he didn't even pay attention to me. I might as well have been invisible." A loud chuckle came from the center of the man's chest. "I pushed a broom across the floor just a few feet away from him as he opened that locker."

Eyes open in eagerness, Mibs leaned forward. "Did you see anything important? Was there any indication that my idea about the break-in at Shelly's Cleaners and the attempted break-in here could be connected with that key?"

He rubbed his hands together and smiled like a Cheshire cat. "I think the guy wanted the key to avoid missing a scheduled business deal. He was likely infuriated when he couldn't get that key until he was able to pick up his laundry from Shelly's."

"A business deal?"

"Yep. It seemed to me like the guy's selling fake driver's licenses to teens." The PI leaned forward. "Several times, I saw him hand various young people a card that appeared to be a driver's license after the kid gave him money."

"I just remembered something Jace said to me a couple weeks ago," Mibs recalled the previous conversation. "He said there had been an influx of underage drinking. They had two separate car accidents where the teenage driver was intoxicated. When the police followed up at the places where the kids had bought the booze, each owner swore that the buyer had a license showing that they were over twenty-one."

"Do you think this guy is connected to this increase in teen drinking?"

"*Private Investigator*, Macey Buckmore," Mibs proclaimed emphatically, "I think you may have found the first real lead in this investigation." She pulled her cell from her pocket and called Jace.

Jace answered on the second ring. "Mibs, are you all right? Are those men still there?"

"Everything is fine. Dasher and Gage have already left. We can talk about that later." She gave Macey an appreciative smile and used Jace's official title. "Detective Lieutenant Trueblood, I have someone that may be a big help in solving the case concerning the fake driver's licenses and the recent break-ins."

Silence filled the line for a few seconds. "Okay, Mibs. What kind of Sherlock Holmes activities have you been up to lately?"

"Oh, not just me. I've had help following up on a hunch." She gave Macey a thumbs-up signal. "Jace, if you aren't too busy to talk to him, can I send my friend to the station tomorrow to fill you in on the information he's uncovered?"

"Go ahead and send him over. Tell him to have the desk sergeant direct him to my office."

"He should be there first thing tomorrow morning?" Mibs paused and gave Macey a questioning glance.

Macey nodded, letting her know that he would be there.

"By the way…do I know who I'll be speaking with?"

"Yes, you know Mr. Buckmore. Talk to you later, honey." Mibs hung up the phone before he could ask for details. She relayed the instructions to Macey. "Tell the desk sergeant that Lieutenant Trueblood is expecting you."

"I surely will," the PI said, his chest puffed up as he headed out of the office.

~~

After the private investigator left, Mibs reviewed the remaining work list with Mary and Deanna. Having Deanna working full-time and taking over tracking inventory freed up time for Mibs and Bernie. They were planning on teaching Deanna the ordering process too. That would leave Mibs more time to devote to requests for custom-made outfits and to begin working on her wedding dress.

"I'll leave things in your capable hands," Mibs told the two ladies. "I need to make a phone call, so I'm going upstairs. Call if you need me for anything before you close up."

As she stepped into her apartment, Mibs felt a wave of exhaustion sweep over her. The work of running the shop hadn't been bad, but the mental and emotional strain of the last couple of days had been exceptionally draining. She dragged herself into the tiny galley kitchen and started a half-pot of coffee brewing. Opening one of the overhead cabinet doors, Mibs pulled out a bag of miniature chocolate bars. By the time she'd poured a mug of coffee and added cream, the overtaxed young woman had devoured three mini-chocolates. She carried the cup and the bag of candy to the sofa, plopped down, and pushed the fourth button on her phone's speed dial.

"Hi, Mibs," Whitney's enthusiastic voice answered. "How are you? Have you picked out a dress? Have you gotten the DNA results yet? Talk to me, friend."

"I will," Mibs said, "if you give me a chance to get in a word."

"Okay. Okay. I'm listening."

Mibs reviewed the day's happenings. Giving Whitney a complete rundown of what was said and done. Just voicing the emotional, life-changing information that had rained down on her seemed to help. "Whitney," she said, her voice trembling, "I'm scared."

"I guess I would be, too," Whitney said. "But just remember, the people who love you will be right by your side. Aunt Bernie and Jace will support you all the way, and so will I."

The two friends talked for a long time. The conversation was therapeutic, helping Mibs regain a sense of equilibrium and calmness. Whitney finally changed the subject, surprising her former college roommate with an unexpected offer. It was actually more of an order.

After listening to the proposition, Mibs hesitated. "I don't know, Whitney. I'd never considered that. I've always thought that I'd make my own wedding dress if I ever got married."

"I know that you could design something fabulous, and it would be beautiful on you. But I would love, love, love to go shopping for a wedding dress and a bridesmaid's dress. My mother knows all the best places. We'd have such a fabulous time! Even though Aunt Bernie would be unlikely to come, you could still ask her and get her input. Jace's mother could also come." Whitney paused before continuing. "Since you and Jace aren't waiting until spring for the wedding, you don't have all that much time."

"Well, I had planned on having several months to design and work on the dress. Of course, moving the wedding to February does rush my plans a bit. But still, I don't know...."

"Mibs," Whitney's voice bubbled with excitement. "Jace's mother likes the idea, too."

"Wait a minute," Mibs muttered. "What do you mean Anna Trueblood likes the idea, too?"

"Oh, umm," the helpful maid of honor cleared her throat. "You gave her my number so we could plan the wedding shower together. This idea kind of, sort of, came up during our conversation."

"Whitney Morgan, you are incorrigible."

"I may be, but I still want us to do this. It will do you good to get away."

Mibs didn't answer right away. It had just dawned on her that when Whitney had first answered the call, she had barely been able to keep herself from crying. Now, her pushy, overbearing, *marvelous* friend had her ready to laugh. "Let me talk to Aunt Bernie before I give you an answer. But I will give a definite, maybe. It would be nice to take a couple days off. And if I don't find something I like, I can rush home and start sewing."

Whitney let out a loud breath. "Thank goodness. Now, I won't have to tell Mom to cancel the reservations we made at several bridal shops."

"What reservations?" Mibs growled.

"Oh, did I say that out loud?"

Mibs turned her eyes upward and shook her

head. "Whitney, why do you and Jace make plans for me before I agree to them?"

"We're just trying to find ways to make you happy," the girl responded, "because we love you."

Mibs chuckled. "When are the reservations?"

Chapter 16

The following day, the desired warrants were waiting for Jace when he returned to the police station. He'd given his detectives an order to pick up the suspects for additional questioning. Jace had already gotten approval for overtime. He hated to ask his team to work on the weekend, but a murder investigation was a priority in the homicide division.

Copies of the shoe's imprint found on the chair were on hand for comparison.

"Lieutenant Trueblood." His new assistant, Carla, stuck her head in, motioning with a thumb pointed over her shoulder. "There is a gentleman here who says you're expecting him. His name is Macey Buckmore."

"Send him in, Carla." Jace stood to greet the local investigator.

"Detective Trueblood," a booming voice filled the room. "Howdy!"

"Mr. Buckmore, please have a seat." Jace sat back down behind his desk. "What have you and my girl, Mibs, been up to?"

A surreptitious expression crossed the robust face. "Miss Monahan and I think you should send some of your officers over to the bus station. And see what's going on at locker 57."

Sitting back, Jace studied the PI. "I recon' you better explain that statement to me."

"Why, I think that young lady was right about the key being connected to the break-ins and fake teen IDs."

"The key?" Jace was still pondering why Mibs had sent Buckmore to talk to him. "Let's try again. What do a key and the bus station have to do with break-ins and fake driver's licenses?"

The two men talked for the next twenty minutes. Macey Buckmore explained Mibs' hunch about the key and his investigative activity at the bus station. Jace listened with interest.

Instead of simply thanking Macey and sending him on his way, Jace decided to reward his successful efforts by asking the private investigator if he'd like to take part in further surveillance. "Mr. Buckmore, I realize that you've been an investigator for many years; however, you are not part of the Havendale Police Force. Therefore, you are still considered a civilian, and I can't have you in harm's way. But if you want to go along as a consultant, I'll arrange it…as long as you promise to do exactly what my officers say." Jace leaned forward.

"Why, I surely would be glad to do that." Buckmore nodded eagerly.

Jace pushed a button on the interoffice phone and waited for his assistant to answer.

"Yes, Lieutenant?" Carla responded.

"According to the schedule I just checked, Officer Schroeder is working the afternoon shift today. Will you please call down to the patrol unit's duty desk and ask their sergeant if I can borrow her awhile?"

"Yes, sir. I'll do that right now." She paused. "By the way, two of the detectives have arrived with the men they picked up."

"Thanks. Tell them I'll join them soon."

Turning back to Macey Buckmore, Jace made a suggestion. "Mr. Buckmore, why don't I show you the break room. You can get a soda or coffee while we wait for the officers who'll be working with you."

"That'd surely be fine." It was evident from Macey's smile that he was delighted to be included in the case.

After leaving the investigator in the break area, Jace headed to the interview rooms.

Juan Mendoza and Eve Clearwater were already there with their charges. Gene Delgado had been sent to pick up Patrick Clyde. Borne and Mosely were seated along the wall outside one of the interview rooms; the four chairs between prevented them from talking to each other.

"Eve." Jace motioned her away from the suspects.

"Yes, Lieutenant?"

"Let Juan keep an eye on these men. I'd like to have you take over another case."

"Whatever you need," she responded.

Turning to Mendoza, Jace informed him that he planned to send Detective Clearwater on another assignment. He could get started on the shoe comparisons as soon as Delgado arrived.

As Clearwater and Trueblood headed through the bullpen, Officer Martha Schroeder entered the area. Jake signaled for her to come forward. Jace directed the group to his office and asked Carla to escort Buckmore from the break room. Jace spent the next half hour coordinating a plan with the two women officers and the private investigator.

Jace wasn't bothered so much because young people might sometimes sneak drinks. He was more concerned that they would drink and then drive, thus, putting themselves and others in harm's way. A seventeen-year-old involved in the last DUI incident was still in the hospital, recovering from multiple injuries. Another seventeen-year-old, who'd died in a drunk driving accident, had been buried three weeks ago. Jace didn't want anyone else hurt because of the sale of alcohol to minors. It was time to put a stop to this.

Macey would resume his undercover act as a maintenance man at the bus station. Schroeder and Clearwater would change to civilian clothes and pose as friends waiting for a bus.

Buckmore had told them that he'd observed the money-for-license exchange; both times, it had been at around 3:45. It wasn't surprising that time was chosen since school would have been out for the day by then. The plan was to signal the officers when he saw the suspect heading for locker 57. Clearwater and Schroeder would wait until they witnessed a transaction—money and a counterfeit license being exchanged. Then they could step in and make an arrest. Since it was now Saturday, the group was uncertain if the twenty-something young man in question would do any business today. The decision was made to set up surveillance for several hours today. If no one showed up, they would reschedule and head to the bus station around two-thirty on Monday.

Buckmore was headed over there now, and the other two would show up shortly after him. Hopefully, an arrest will be made, if not today, within the next several days.

When Jace made his way back to the interview area, Detective Delgado was seating Patrick Clyde. The three men remained on the chairs in the hallway. Juan Mendoza directed each of them to take off their right shoe. After a few questioning glances and one, 'What?' Mosely, Borne, and Clyde removed the requested shoe. None of them matched the copy of the impression from the museum's chair.

Stepping forward, Jace handed a search warrant to each museum employee. "This search warrant covers your work lockers, homes, and cars."

"What the heck?" Patrick Clyde scanned the warrant. "What are you hoping to find?"

Jace watched for any facial reactions when he made the statement, "It appears that Roger Patterson's killer stood on a chair the night he committed the murder."

Confused expressions popped up on both Mosely's and Clyde's faces. After an almost imperceptible flash of surprise shot through Albert Borne's eyes, the man's face went blank. He stared straight ahead, didn't ask any questions, or make any comments. His lack of response caught Jace's attention.

"You think one of us killed Roger?" Clyde questioned, peering up at Delgado, the detective who'd brought him to the station. "Why would any of us do that? What would be our motive?"

Juan watched Jace for a signal. Seeing Jace's nod to proceed, he told the suspects about the thefts and the replacements with forgeries.

Again, there was no noticeable change in the countenance of Borne's features. As with the other two men, Jace expected some kind of reaction. Unlike Albert Borne, the other two employees both showed surprise and disbelief.

Although they weren't ready to rule out the other men, Borne's lack of reaction, coupled with the unexplained cash deposits in his bank account, moved him to the top of the suspect list.

"Gentlemen," Jace addressed the group, "you have a choice of staying here while we search your premises, or you can go with the officers to your home. If you go with them, you will have to stand aside and follow their orders."

"Search away," Clyde said. "I don't have anything to hide." He glanced up and down the hallway. "Do I have to stay sitting here? Can I get a sandwich? I'm hungry."

Detective Delgado motioned toward the interview room with a table and two chairs. "You can wait in there, and I'll send somebody out to get you some food."

"I better go with you," Nick Mosely, the art handler and most senior employee of Tuppence Museum, responded. "My wife is home, and it'll probably scare her if the police suddenly show up."

"What about you, Mr. Borne?" Jace queried. "Can we get you anything, or would you like to accompany the officers to your house?"

"Actually, Detective Trueblood, I have a

meeting that I don't want to miss or reschedule. What if I meet you at my house in an hour?" Borne stood up, buttoning his caramel-colored wool topcoat.

"Perhaps, in the meantime, you could search my locker at work. Just like my coworkers, I have nothing to hide."

"All right, Mr. Borne," said Jace, "as long as you're sure the meeting won't take over an hour. My men will catch up with you at your place."

As soon as the three men stood up and headed to their various destinations, Detective Delgado turned to Juan Mendoza. "Is Lieutenant Trueblood really letting Borne have time to leave and possibly hide evidence?"

"Not likely," Juan replied with confidence, "Jace knows what he'd doing."

Overhearing the two detectives, Jace smirked as he pulled out his phone and called the detective division's desk sergeant. The call was answered on the second ring.

"Brice, this is Jace." Giving Sergeant Long the description of Albert Borne and informing him that the man was on his way out, Jace told him what he wanted.

"If you call down now, we can have a couple plain-clothed men from robbery waiting when he leaves the building. Make sure they keep him in their sight but don't let him see them following. I have a feeling he's heading to his home to hide or remove evidence. They need to make sure he doesn't take anything out of the house or anywhere else he may stop. If he goes to his own address, the officers should wait

until he comes out, stop him, and hold him until
I get there. I'll bring a team with me to help
search his house."

Chapter 17

As Lieutenant Trueblood had suspected, Albert Borne headed straight to his home. The undercover car drove past the house before pulling to the curb. Officers Iverson and Nugent from the robbery division kept an eye on Borne as he climbed out of his vehicle and entered his house. As soon as he entered the building, the two men backed their car up and pulled in front of Borne's sedan. They hurried to the edge of the suspect's property. Officer Iverson stationed himself behind some bushes close to the front door.

Detective Nugent made his way around to the back, staying out of the view of the windows. As he reached the back corner of the house and slipped behind a tree, he heard a door slam. Worried that the suspect may be leaving through the back door, Nugent quickly peered around the tree.

Borne was not there. The man wasn't on the steps or anywhere in the yard. Scanning the sidewalk, alley, and nearby homes, the detective spotted an older lady gazing at him from across the narrow alleyway. Nugent suspected that it was her door that he'd heard shutting as she'd brought her dog out. A black and white Boston Terrier tugged on the leash, nudging at something in the grass. The officer nodded at the stooped, gray-haired woman wearing a faded house dress and fuzzy slippers.

She didn't respond, just continued to stare, puckering her lips in a disapproving manner. He turned away from her and set his eyes on Borne's back door.

~~

Officer Iverson, who'd positioned himself where he'd have a good view of the front, had checked his watch. Twelve minutes after Borne had entered the house, he came out. As soon as the suspect stepped off the porch, Iverson moved into the open and held out his badge.

"Albert Borne, I'm Officer Iverson from the HPD. Lieutenant Trueblood directed us to have you wait here until he arrives."

Iverson had expected him to show defiance or perhaps anger, but the only expression he noticed was annoyance.

"I told Detective Trueblood that I'd meet him here in about an hour. I have a meeting scheduled. I just stopped here to freshen up first."

"Your meeting will have to wait." Iverson called Nugent and told him that he had Borne.

Nugent had just reached the sidewalk when Lieutenant Trueblood's Chevy Silverado pulled up. Jace and uniformed officer, Bret Clarkson, climbed out of the truck.

"I was just telling this man...." Borne flicked his hand toward Nugent... "I'd just stopped home to freshen up before my meeting."

"Is that right?" Trueblood questioned. "Are you sure you didn't come here to hide evidence? A pair of shoes, perhaps?"

Without batting an eye, Borne replied, "Don't be ridiculous. I told you I have nothing to hide.

Go ahead, do your search. You won't be able to find anything."

"Which is it, *Mr. Borne?*" Jace stepped close and glared at him. "You have nothing to hide, or now that you've hidden it, you don't think we'll be able to find anything?"

The suspect's only reply was a condescending smirk.

Two squad cars pulled up to the curb, and a van holding a crew of crime scene technicians soon followed.

"Officers Iverson and Nugent, can I impose on you one more time?" Trueblood asked.

"Sure," the tall, thin Iverson answered. "What do you need, Lieutenant?"

"Can you take Mr. Borne back to the station and have Sergeant Long hold him for questioning on the death of Roger Patterson and theft from the Tuppence Museum?"

"No problem." The officer looked at the suspect sternly. "It'll be my pleasure."

Trueblood had started to turn away but pivoted back around. "Wait a minute." Gesturing to Clarkson, he said, "Brett, pass me one of those copies."

Pulling out a photocopy of the shoe imprint, Officer Clarkson handed it to the lieutenant.

Trueblood pointed to Borne's shoe. "It wouldn't be beyond the realm of possibility that you might have changed shoes while in the house. Since we already checked the shoe you were wearing at the station, there's a chance we wouldn't check again."

"Ha, that's clever; most police wouldn't have thought of that." The suspect seemed almost impressed. "But, alas, I'm still wearing the same pair of shoes."

Trueblood checked to make sure before sending him with the robbery division team.

"You'll be hearing from my lawyer!" Borne shouted as the door of the unmarked car began closing. "The Havendale Police Force and you personally, *Trueblood*, will be sued for every penny you have."

~~

While watching the assembly of searchers heading toward the house, Jace instructed Clarkson to ensure the team had the shoe imprint image. However, two hours of searching revealed nothing of significance.

None of the several pairs of shoes matched the impression. No jewelry-making equipment was found—nothing incriminating other than bank statements confirming what they had already uncovered. The team had even pushed on walls, searched for hidden panels, checked the floors for loose boards, and worked their way through the attic and basement. The officers and technicians seemed ready to wind up their search. But, Jace said, "Search again. Top to bottom. And cover the outside again, too. Don't forget the garbage cans." There was a collective sigh as the search continued.

Slowly walking from room to room, Jace carefully ran his eyes over everything in view. He thought about how the murder weapon had been hidden in plain sight in the museum's weapons room, and he wondered if they were trying too hard. Maybe the same reasoning was used in suppressing evidence in this house.

Jace eventually found himself pacing back and forth in the basement. Todd Benson watched him as he studied the cement and panel area.

"I know you mentioned shoes and jewelry, but you appear to be searching for something specific," Benson said. "Would you care to fill me in? What are you considering?"

Jace cut his eyes over to the lead crime scene investigator. "Something obvious, Todd. Something staring us in the face, which we just aren't seeing."

Benson murmured, "Okay. Something that stands out but we may not notice. Hmm." With his arms crossed over his chest, the investigator tapped his fingers against his upper arms as his eyes scanned the low-ceilinged room. Suddenly, focusing on the furnace, he called out. "Jace, would that be an example of what you're talking about?"

Jace stepped up to the crime scene tech and looked in the direction Benson pointed. "What do you see?"

"The pipes on the furnace, the ones on the water heater, too. They're all old, dulled, and brown from age. I'd say they've been there for years." Moving closer, Benson scrutinized the attached PVC pipes. "All except the ones across the back of the furnace, which appear to be new. I'd say they were recently added."

Jace studied the surrounding floor. He made his way behind the furnace. "Benson, you're a genius."

"Of course I am," Benson tilted his head. "But would you mind telling me why or how?"

Jace didn't answer. He'd already moved to the

wall and began pressing on the paneling mounted behind the furnace. "The furnace has been slid forward about three feet. Do you see those light scratches on the floor? The new pipes were added as extensions." The detective tapped on the wall, stopped, and glanced back, smiling. "Todd, it sounds hollow behind this panel. Help me see if there is some kind of door."

It took only a few minutes to figure out that a panel slid into the wall when pushed to the right, revealing a four-foot by six-foot area. Aiming a flashlight into the tiny room, they saw a chain for a pull light hanging from the ceiling. When Jace yanked the chain, a LED shop light flooded the area with brightness, more than enough light to illuminate a desk. The desk was littered with jeweler's tools and an assortment of stones that were likely synthetic stones, glass, and cubic zirconia gemstones. There was also a long, slender box holding silver and gold-colored metal threads.

"Well, I'll be flabbergasted," Todd Benson muttered.

Jace conducted a thorough search in and around the desk in case Albert Borne had stashed a pair of shoes in this secret room. Stepping out of the close quarters, he addressed Benson, "I'll let you and your boys tag and bag this stuff. I know you'll get detailed pictures."

Jace continued the conversation more to himself than to the technician. "Okay, Borne, we have you for the forgeries. But you're not going to worm your way out of the murder charge." Growling, he shook his head. "Where did you put those shoes?" The detective suspected that the murderer's shoe would have the same trace of Patterson's blood found on the chair. That would be solid proof. *But where was the shoe?*

It was past eight in the evening when Jace instructed the police personnel to close up shop. Ensuring the property was well-marked with crime scene tape, he gave instructions to keep a guard on the house's front and one on the back. The garbage wasn't even to be collected. No one was to go in or out until the search for the possibly incriminating shoe continued in the morning.

Earlier, Jace spoke with Detectives Mendoza and Delgado. They had followed up on the other places listed on the warrants. Searching the properties belonging to Mosely and Clyde turned up nothing.

Eve Clearwater had reported in at 6:30 p.m. There had been no activity at the bus station. The trio of Clearwater, Schroeder, and Buckmore made arrangements to be back there Monday afternoon.

Climbing into his truck, Jace relaxed against the seat, the activity and stress of the day brought on a bout of weariness, and he was definitely hungry. He pulled out his cell phone and called Mibs. Some of the tension slipped away as soon as he heard her voice.

"Hi, sweetheart. I'll stop and pick up Shadow in a little bit. Are there any leftovers that y'all want to get rid of, or should I stop and pick up somethin' when I head home?"

"We had sandwiches and fruit for supper. I'll

fix you a sandwich if you'd like. Or, if you'd rather, I can whip up an omelet. I have mushrooms, onions, pepper, and cheese to jazz it up."

"An omelet?" Jace perked up. "That would be nice."

"I could even add some French Toast if you like."

"That sounds really good, but I'll probably just eat and run. I'm expectin' another busy day tomorrow."

"This day wore me out, too."

"I reckon it did." Jace paused before he added, "Darlin', I was so lucky the day I met you."

Mibs surprised him with a soft peal of laughter. "As I remember it, we didn't exactly start off on the most amicable terms the day we met."

Jace smiled to himself, and he had to agree. "Yeah. I remember that you informed me I wasn't doing my job right; I needed to check all the evidence again. I thought you were a bit stubborn and pushy."

"And, at first, I thought you were obnoxious and unapproachable," Mibs quipped back. "So...is that how you'd describe me now?"

"Now, I would call you sweet, kind-hearted, beautiful, and the best thing in my life."

"Hmm." Laughter could be detected in her voice. "So you wouldn't use those first descriptions anymore?"

He chuckled, "I didn't say that. You're still stubborn, determined, and unafraid to speak your mind."

"Oh?"

"But now I see those as good qualities. I wouldn't change a thing about you."

Mibs was silent for a few beats. "I love you, Jace; I love my determined detective. I love my caring and handsome fiancé."

Jace started the truck and sighed. It was surprising how a few minutes of talking to his girl made some of the tension leave his shoulders, and the ache that had tried to settle in his head began to fade. "I'll be there in a few minutes."

"Okay. Drive carefully, honey."

Chapter 18

"You're here bright and early," Sergeant Long greeted Jace as he entered the bullpen at 7:15 a.m.

"Morn', Brice." A yawn escaped as he greeted the desk sergeant. Jace had dropped off Shadow early and then attended 6:00 a.m. Mass at Christ the King Church. He knew that Mibs had called the rectory the day before to inform Father Smith and Deacon Miller that they'd have to postpone their first pre-wedding class.

Jace slid a box from the local bakery onto the front desk. "These are compliments of Bernice Monahan. When Mibs told her aunt I worked late and would start again this morning, Bernie had muffins and pastries sent over. She had a box with enough for the whole team waiting when I dropped off Shadow this mornin'."

"Nice." Long opened the box, and the smell of fresh baked goods wafted out into the air. "I'll give her a call and thank her."

"Borne's lawyer asked that we call her this morning before we start questioning him." Long handed over a business card with the lawyer's information.

"Give her a call and inform her that I'll have the suspect in the interview room this morning by 9:00."

After getting through the requisite paperwork and answering several emails, Jace called down to the robbery division, asking if Nugent and Iverson were in the office today.

They were. The two detectives would come to talk to him in a while.

Jace pressed a button on the interoffice communication system. When Carla answered, he said, "Carla, as soon as Detective Mendoza gets here, please have him come see me."

"Will do, Lieutenant."

"Oh, by the way, Carla, thanks for coming in today."

"No problem."

Since it was Sunday, Jace had requested but not demanded that his team come in today. Most of them were planning on heading into the station.

A few minutes later, Eve Clearwater stepped into the doorway. "Lieutenant."

"Come on in." Jace pointed to a chair. "What's up?"

"I wanted to touch base on the fake driver's license assignment."

"I understand that nothing happened yesterday."

"That's correct. We figure that guy with counterfeit licenses doesn't do business every day. We're planning on staking out the terminal Monday. How long should we keep the surveillance up?"

Drumming his fingers on the top of his desk, Jace considered the situation. "Let me make a call." He pulled out his police-issued phone and called Captain Taylor. After a short conversation, he hung up and turned back to the detective.

"The captain is giving us permission to keep Martha Schroeder on the assignment through the next week if needed. By then, we should have some results or know what kind of schedule the suspect keeps. Since the school doesn't let out until after 3:00, you and Officer Schroeder should go with your plan of being in place by 2:30. Use your judgment as to how long you think you should stay in the evenings. If we haven't been able to make an arrest by Friday night, we may want to rethink our strategy."

"Jace." Detective Mendoza came into the room. "Carla said you wanted to see me."

"Come in, Juan." Jace turned back to the other detective. "Eve, you coordinate with Martha and Macey. You're lead on the assignment." Leaning back, he added, "After you set things up with the other two, join us near the interview room."

Detective Clearwater returned to her desk. Jace and Juan reviewed the previous day's search warrants' results. Plans were made to head back over to Borne's home after the interview.

"I hope Borne decides to cooperate," Jace said. "I still think that once he knew we had a print of the killer's shoe, he went to his house to hide that pair. It took us half a day to find that hidden panel in the basement where we located the jeweler's stuff. But I haven't given up on finding the shoes. The detectives who followed him reported that he didn't bring anything with him when he came out of the house."

The interoffice system buzzed, and Jace answered. "Yes, Carla."

"Two officers from the robbery division are here to see you."

~~

Mibs finished up the community theater's Renaissance-style costume. She had gone to Mass with Bernie before attacking the final details on the dress. She tried not to use Sunday for what she considered work: mending, sales, or stocking shelves. But doing creative things, which she enjoyed, wasn't a chore. Instead, it was a pleasure and relaxing when she added creative touches to an outfit or pieced a quilt together for herself or for a personal gift.

"What do you think, Aunt Bernie?" Mibs ran her eyes over the dress as she straightened the edge of a sleeve. "I think it turned out nicely."

Aunt Bernie adjusted her glasses and reviewed Mibs' work. She leaned on her cane as she gave her approval. "It's beautiful and well made. Excellent job, my dear."

"I took careful measurements of both the ladies who will be wearing the two outfits, so I'll be surprised if they need more than minor adjustments." Mibs removed the costume from the dressmaking dummy and carefully folded it, placing it into a tissue-lined box.

Aunt Bernie accompanied Mibs to the front of the store, where Mibs slid the box from her hand onto the top of the one already sitting on the 'finished items' shelf.

The soft jingle of the bells above the door announced the entrance of Bernie's two friends,

Marge and Hazel. Bernie had left the door unlocked.

Seventy-nine years old, Marge, the youngest of the trio, had her hands full with two bags from the Blueberry Café. Aunt Bernie told Mibs that the ladies were having brunch in the break area, followed by a game of pinochle.

"You know where the table is, girls," Bernie said. "I have everything set up, and I'll be there in a minute."

Shadow stayed by Bernie's side, even though the enticing smells coming from the food containers had the dog's eyes following Marge.

"Go ahead, Shadow. I know you're going to mooch some tidbits from us." Bernie pointed to the back and signaled the Belgium Malinois to go.

"Oh, Aunt Bernie, you spoil that dog." Mibs shook her head.

"Of course I do." Her aunt was unapologetic. "Are you sure you don't want to join us?"

"No, thank you. I'm going to spend some time sorting through back copies of magazines that have piled up during the last couple of months." She added, "Besides, I can't keep up with you three when you play cards."

The two Monahan ladies turned to the door when it opened again. A slim, strawberry-blond woman wearing a well-fitted Gucci chalk-striped wool suit stepped into the room.

When Aunt Bernie saw the girl, a mirror image of Mibs, she froze.

Mibs gasped as she studied the lookalike silhouetted in the doorway. "Camilla?" Mibs said so quietly, her voice barely carried across the room.

Taking hesitant steps, the green-eyed girl stopped when she was a few feet away from her carbon copy. She lifted her hand, palm up, and murmured, "Clara?"

Mibs moved to fill the last few feet between them and held her hand out. She instinctively placed her palm on top of the one waiting in front of her. "Everyone calls me Mibs."

Although it was not more than ten seconds, time seemed to stand still as the two girls stared at each other.

Taking a deep breath, Mibs glanced down at their touching hands before her eyes moved to seek out her beloved aunt. "Aunt Bernie..." She had to take a breath before she could continue to speak. "...Aunt Bernie, I believe this is Camilla Richmond."

Camilla squared her shoulders and walked with perfect posture towards the counter. "You must be Bernice Monahan. It is a pleasure to meet you."

"Hello, Miss Richmond." Aunt Bernie seemed to study the young woman.

There was an uncomfortable pause; uncertainty hung in the air. Then, finally, Bernie broke the silence. "Mibs, perhaps you and Miss Richmond would like to go up to your apartment and talk."

"Aunt Bernie?" Since her aunt had been the main person in her life for so long, Mibs knew that Aunt Bernie would understand the various questions she asked with just the speaking of her name. *Aunt Bernie, are you okay? Are you ready for this astronomical change in our lives?*

Will it be all right?

Aunt Bernie lovingly smiled. "The Lord has a reason for everything that happens. Go, meet your sister." Waving her hand in a shooing motion, she repeated, "Go."

Chapter 19

"Thank you for coming up," Jace said, "and for your help yesterday."

Nugent and Iverson adjusted the two chairs in front of the lieutenant's desk and sat down. Nugent said, "Glad we could help. Actually, since part of this case deals with stolen antiques, we think that we may be of even more help."

Jace's brows rose. "Yeah? Talk to me."

Iverson explained. "We could use the robbery department's resources to try and see if any of the jewelry was sold by one of our listed dealers known for fencing stolen items. If we find anything, we might be able to find out who sold it to them."

Jace sat forward. "What do you need?"

"Descriptions of the stolen pieces." Iverson said, "Preferably pictures."

Jace hit the button for Carla's desk. When she answered, he asked, "Could you make copies of the pictures of the jewelry missing from the Jeffery Tuppence Museum? Make sure and include the descriptions, please."

"I'll bring them to your office in a few minutes."

Turning back to Iverson and Nugent, Jace said, "Now I have a question about yesterday."

"What's that?" Nugent asked.

"You said that Albert Borne went into the house, stayed twelve minutes, and didn't bring anything out with him. Correct?"

"That's right."

"Are you sure that he didn't go out back while you were heading to his house?'

Nugent hesitated before replying. "I can't swear to that, Lieutenant, but I don't think he did. I heard what sounded like a door closing. I only took a minute to get to the back after hearing the noise. Borne was not outside when I scanned the yard. Like I said yesterday, a neighbor lady had brought her dog outside. I figured it was her shutting a door that I heard."

"Okay." Jace ran his hand through his hair as he considered the man's words.

Carla brought in the requested information and placed it on Jace's desk. He handed the folders to Officer Iverson and thanked the men for any help they could give him.

A few minutes before nine, Jace headed to the interrogation room to begin questioning Albert Borne. When the lawyer showed up, Borne would be presented with burglary and theft charges, along with suspicion of murder. Detective Mendoza met Jace at the door of the assigned room, and the suspect was escorted in by an officer a few minutes later.

Borne was seated in a hard chair behind a solid metal desk. The door was shut, and the suspect was left alone. Jace knew it wouldn't take Borne long to realize that the chair was slightly off-kilter. One front leg of the chair was half an inch shorter than the two back legs. The other front leg was an additional fraction of an inch shorter, just enough to make sitting a little uncomfortable. The homicide team never bothered to bring that fact to a suspect's attention.

At precisely 9:00 a.m., the sharp click of high heels could be heard echoing down the hall. A local defense attorney, Rita Yates, approached the two lawmen waiting outside the interview room. The navy blue suit and no-nonsense short haircut style presented a professional appearance.

"Ms. Yates." Jace nodded as he reached over and turned the doorknob.

The lawyer entered. Jace and Juan stepped in after her, and the door closed with a loud click. Juan lifted a chair from near the wall and placed it on the suspect's side of the table.

"Please, take a seat, ma'am. Mr. Borne has been read his rights," Juan told her.

The two detectives sat down across from Borne and his lawyer. Jace opened the small cardboard box he'd brought into the room. As he slowly lifted out pictures taken of the secret hideaway in Borne's basement and placed them in front of him, the lieutenant watched the suspect's face for a reaction. His smug, superior expression didn't change.

"What are these?" Yates asked as she leaned forward to study the photos.

"Proof," Jace said calmly. "Enough proof to charge your client with theft."

The lawyer glanced toward Albert Borne. She whispered in his ear. Instead of replying to her question, Borne peered at Jace.

"Detective Trueblood, these pictures don't prove anything except the fact that I like to make costume jewelry in my spare time."

Ms. Yates tried to whisper something to her client again, but he waved her away.

"I'm paying you plenty of money. Do your job and get me out of here. I can't believe I've already spent a night in jail." With an arrogant expression, the man sat back, glowering each time the chair wobbled.

"What about the thin gold- and silver- coated wires, which were also found in your house?" Jace slid the picture of the narrow box of wires closer to the suspect. "They've been sent to the lab for analysis. The chances are pretty good that their composition will exactly match the wires used to make the dagger that stabbed Roger Patterson."

A slight movement of his mouth and a quick squinting of his eyes were minor telltale signs of reaction.

"Just because my client had wires, which may or may not match those used to make some weapon, does not prove he stole anything. Nor that he committed a murder."

"Oh, I'm not sure a judge and jury would agree with you, Ms. Yates." Jace shrugged and tapped the set of pictures. "We've also sent the glass gems and semiprecious stones collected from your client's hidden room to the lab. They will be compared to the stones used in the forged jewelry found at Tuppence Museum."

When the suspect once again plastered a stolid expression on his face, Juan asked, "Didn't we tell you, Borne, that we contacted an appraisal specialist? He came down and examined every piece of jewelry in the museum. He found several forgeries."

Smirking, Borne jutted his chin forward. "Perhaps you can charge me with theft, but you don't possibly have enough evidence to make a murder charge stick."

Jace sat back and folded his arms across his chest. "You had the means and opportunity to make that dagger. If the analysis of the wires matches the murder weapon, I think you will be charged with killing Roger Patterson."

There was a bit of worry in Ms. Yates' eyes.

Jace nodded. "Of course, when we find that pair of shoes, there won't be any doubt of your conviction."

"What shoes?" Yates questioned. She turned to Borne. "What pair of shoes is the detective talking about?"

The bored attitude returned as he nonchalantly answered, "He has some crazy idea that the killer left a footprint at the scene. But, even if that *were* true, I'm certain he won't find any shoe connected to me."

A loud knock reverberated across the small room. Juan stood and opened the door, accepting the paperwork Sergeant Long handed him. He passed the papers to Jace, who scanned them before giving them to the lawyer.

"You'll want to read through these charges. Notification of when the arraignment is scheduled will be sent to you." Jace motioned for Juan to follow him out. "We'll leave you two alone to talk a bit before the prisoner is taken back to his cell." Moving toward the door, he added, "Ms. Yates, if you have any questions, you can leave them with the desk sergeant, and he'll see we get them."

Jace and Juan stepped out and closed the door. Captain Taylor and Detective Clearwater joined them. They'd been watching through the two-way mirror in the next room.

"What do you think, Hank?" Jace asked his boss.

"We've got a solid case for burglary and theft." Taylor slowly nodded. "And probably the murder. It would really cinch it if we could find a shoe to match that impression on the chair."

"Yeah, especially if, as I suspect, there's still a trace of blood clinging to the treads in the outer sole." He shifted his focus between his two detectives. "Was there a thorough search for those shoes done at the museum and in Borne's car?"

"Yes, sir," Eve assured him as Juan gave an affirmative nod.

"Eve, Gene Delgado plans on showing up around 10:00. When he gets here, how 'bout you two make sure that all the trash cans and alleys along the way were checked. Drive the route Borne would have taken from the police station to his house. If anywhere appears to have the slightest possibility of being a good place to toss them, please search. Then search again."

"Okay, Jace, we'll take care of it," Eve replied.

Captain Taylor stared at the lead detectives. "So, you think Borne may have thrown the shoes someplace after leaving the station?"

"Truthfully, Hank, I don't. But I still believe in checking all possibilities. I have a gut feeling that they're on his property. If not inside the house, then outside." After contemplating the situation for a minute, Jace smiled. "I wonder if we might have a witness who could help us – if we asked nicely."

Captain Taylor shook his head. "I don't know what you have in mind, but when you get that expression on your face, I've found it best to just let you go with your hunch. It usually pays off in the end." Heading down the hall, Taylor waved. "Let me know if you find anything new."

"Juan, you and I are going back to Borne's neighborhood." Jace headed to the bullpen. "On our way, we're going to make a stop. I think the bakery still sells homemade 'puppy' cookies along with the human baked stuff."

"Dog treats?" Juan pondered his words.

Carla cast a surprised glance at Jace when he stopped at her desk and asked, "Carla could you get me a lady's name and her dog's name?"

Chapter 20

Mibs offered Camilla Richmond one of the high-backed stools at the kitchen island in her small apartment. "Would you like something to drink? With the chilly weather outside, something hot might be good. I have coffee, hot chocolate, or tea."

"A cup of tea would be nice," Camilla replied as she sat, placing her Coach leather purse on the edge of the granite countertop.

"Would you prefer black, green, or peppermint?" Mibs turned the burner under the tea kettle on and adjusted the flame.

"I do like peppermint tea."

Opening the cupboard and removing two saucers and two cups, Mibs set them on the island, placing a crystal sugar bowl and matching pitcher with cream next to them. She turned back to the cabinet, opened a utensil drawer, and pulled out two spoons, slipping a spoon on the edge of each saucer.

"I like lemon shortbread with my peppermint tea," Mibs said as she filled a serving dish with the small, flakey cookies. "If you'd like, I have a local clover honey that is excellent for tea."

"I prefer to add cream and sugar," Camilla said. "Mother teases me, saying that is the old English way."

"I drink peppermint tea plain," Mibs explained as she poured the hot water into a ceramic teapot, covering the mesh tea ball infuser filled with peppermint leaves. "With other hot teas, I prefer to stir in a bit of honey." Mibs realized that they were both making small talk. Apparently, neither knew how to start the actual conversation that lingered in their minds. Mibs stepped around the counter and slipped into the seat next to Camilla. Both of the girls remained silent for a couple minutes before speaking.

"*Camilla*," Mibs blurted out at the same time the other girl said, "*Mibs*."

"Please, you go first," Camilla offered.

Mibs took a deep breath and slowly released it. "This is all new to me. Last summer, my friend Whitney sent a picture to me…a picture of you. That was the first time I had any serious thoughts about the possibility of having relatives, people that I never knew existed, but who I was tied to in some familial way." She picked up the teapot and carefully filled the waiting cups. "Even then, I didn't take the idea too seriously. But when my fiancé, Jace, and my friend, Tony, started investigating the girl in Whitney's picture…investigating *you,* things changed. I'm still not sure how I feel." Mibs sighed, lifting her eyes to gaze at her newfound sister. "It's confusing. It still feels unreal."

Sighing again, she picked up her tea, inhaling the aroma of peppermint rising from the rosebud-trimmed china cup. She placed the cup down and continued. "Camilla, did you always know you'd had a sister? A twin? Because I didn't. How would you feel if you were suddenly told that you aren't who you thought you were? If not for some event that happened years ago, your whole life would have been different." She took a moment to pull her confused feelings together. "Please don't misunderstand. I don't regret the wonderful life I've been blessed with. I just…I just don't know what to think."

Camilla Richmond hesitantly placed her hand on top of Mibs' hand as it rested on the counter. "I've known for many years that I was born as a twin. Mother never took down the baby pictures of us taken just a few weeks before you were lost." Taking her hand back, she picked up the cream pitcher and poured a dollop into her tea before adding half a spoon of sugar, stirring gently without touching the side of the cup. "Clara has been a shadow hovering in my life for as long as I can remember."

Camilla hesitated before continuing. "I didn't mean that in the way it possibly sounded. It was not a bad thing. How can I explain what a little girl…what I thought when I was little?" She placed her hands flat on the counter and turned to face Mibs. "I must have been four or five when I wandered into the library and saw Mother holding one of the framed baby pictures. She seemed so unhappy. I walked up to her and tugged on the hem of her dress. When she looked down, I asked her why she was sad. She told me that not knowing what happened to her other baby, Clara, left an ache in her heart. I wanted to know where Clara went. Mother used a simple explanation about some men who took us and hid us. They got me back but couldn't find Clara."

Tears were brimming along the edges of Mibs'

eyes as she pondered Camilla's words. "Did what she said make sense to you at that time?"

Camilla gave a half-hearted chuckle. "I thought that if I could find Clara, then my mother wouldn't be sad. I spent the rest of the afternoon searching the house and the yard. I searched behind every piece of furniture, every drapery, and every tree. I kept calling out, 'Clara, Clara, come out wherever you are!' Finally, my parents realized what I was doing." Smiling and shaking her head, she said, "I remember my father picking me up and pulling me into his arms. He and my mother kept me close the rest of the day, telling me that it wasn't my responsibility to find my sister."

"Hmm," Mibs murmured. "I've been thinking about how all this has affected me. I realize that as parents Crystal and Jackson Richmond must have been devastated. But I hadn't considered what you faced over the years." Mibs lifted the teapot and refilled their cups. "Did you...uh...think of...Clara, as you got older?"

"Oh, yes. Often. For as long as I can remember, whenever I went any place where people were around – stores, parks, theaters – if I saw a girl around my age with light red hair, I'd wonder if she could be my sister." Shrugging, she muttered, "Silly? Right?"

"No, not silly." Mibs studied Camilla. "If I'd known that there was a possibility that I had a sister somewhere, I would have searched too. In fact, maybe it was good that I didn't know." Sitting back, she rubbed her hand across her chin before she confessed, "I seem to have a compulsion to search for answers when I encounter a problem or mystery. It's gotten me into trouble a few times."

A lull in the conversation brought on a companionable silence. The green eyes of the young woman dressed in expensive chic attire stared unfixed across the room as memories wandered through her mind. Strawberry-blond tresses slipped forward as Mibs, dressed in jeans and a comfortable cotton blouse, tilted her head as she tried to process the information she'd heard.

"Why did you come here?" Mibs suddenly asked.

Camilla slowly turned to face her mirror image and replied in a tone that conveyed a 'how could I not come?' attitude. "I had to. I've been half-consciously searching for you all my life. I had to know if you were really my twin sister."

"Am I? Do you know now?"

"We both know. Don't we? I think we knew the moment we saw each other."

"Yes." Mibs smiled. "As soon as I looked into your eyes, I was sure." She let out a deep breath. "I wonder what Mr. and Mrs. Richmond...what your parents...." Mibs scrunched up her face. "I don't know what to call them. I wonder what *they* think."

"With my mother's insistence, father asked for updates every year. I think he really thought you had died soon after being kidnapped. Not that he wanted that. He just couldn't keep hoping." Camilla squeezed Mibs's hand. "Mom never stopped believing that someday they'd find out something. If not find their missing daughter, then at least get some kind of closure." She took a dainty sip from the teacup and glanced back at Mibs. "Lawrence is the one who really doesn't know what to think."

"Lawrence?" Mibs didn't recognize the name. "Who is Lawrence?"

"Oh, you don't know. Lawrence is my brother...ah, our brother."

"Brother?"

Clearing her throat, Camilla nodded. "I just assumed you'd been told. He's nineteen, in the first year of college, and wants to be a doctor like Father."

Mibs ran a hand across her forehead. "Tony left a thick packet for me to go through. He said it had details about the Richmond family. I guess I wasn't ready to open it yet."

Camilla stood up and reached for her purse. "Maybe it would be a good idea if I left, so you could read the information your friend gave you."

"Wait," Mibs said. "When will I see you again?"

Camilla gave her a warm smile. "How about tomorrow?"

"Oh, okay," Mibs muttered.

"When I drove down here today, I hadn't made definite plans. I thought I would meet you. Then, I'd decide to drive back to Metrofield or get a room for the night." Camilla added, "I think we both need a little time. Then, we can talk more."

As they headed down the stairs, Camilla asked if there was a decent hotel nearby.

"Yes. There is a Holiday Inn at the edge of town. Or if you prefer, there are a couple of bed and breakfast places, too."

"The Holiday Inn sounds fine." When they reached the shop's door, Camilla hesitated. "I think that if Father can't persuade you to come up to Metrofield, he will be coming down here within the next few days."

Mibs wasn't sure how to respond, simply uttering, "Oh?"

"Apparently, your fiancé is a lieutenant on the local police force, and he's made it clear that all inquiries should go through him." A twinkle appeared in Camilla's eye as she smiled. "I've known Mark Gage, from Gage Investigations, for quite a few years. He's not used to being put in his place. So I found it amusing when I heard him tell Father about Lieutenant Trueblood's strict instructions concerning you."

Mibs couldn't keep from smiling as she thought about Jace and the stoic, no-nonsense demeanor he could present when he was in his detective, or in her case, protective mode. While other times, her beloved could be gentle, caring, and extremely sweet. Grabbing a pad and pencil from the counter, she asked Camilla to write down her phone number.

"I'll talk to Jace, and perhaps we can arrange a time and place to meet which will work for all of us."

As her sister turned to leave, Mibs called, "Camilla, wait!" Closing the gap between them, she said, "Thank you for coming."

After Camilla left, Mibs decided to check on

the three card-playing seniors. Stepping around the counter, she discovered Shadow sitting by the gate.

"Shadow, are you checking up on me?" She rubbed her hand across the dog's back and praised the pet before continuing to the back room. "So, who's winning?" Mibs questioned Bernie and her friends.

"It's still fairly close," Marge declared.

Aunt Bernie gazed at her niece, apparently trying to judge how the conversation between her and Miss Richmond had gone. "How is everything, my dear? Are you doing okay?"

Marge and Hazel were obviously aware of the circumstance of Camilla's visit. However, they both made a show of pretending to *not listen* as they looked everywhere except at Mibs.

She smiled at her aunt's best friends before answering. "I will be fine, Aunt Bernie." Mibs snagged a finger sandwich and two coconut *petit fours*. "I have some reading to do, so I'll leave you ladies to finish your game." Before leaving, Mibs leaned over and gave her great-aunt a kiss on the cheek.

When she stepped back into her apartment, Mibs set her snack down and purposely walked over to her dresser, where she picked up a large folder. She returned to the counter, slipping the papers from the folder. She began reading slowly, letting her mind absorb the Richmond family story.

Thirty-five minutes later, Clara Richmond, known for twenty-four years as Mirabelle Louise Monahan, let the pages of information she'd just read settle in her mind. She waited for the coffee she had just started to finish dripping into the carafe, and she pondered the fact that her biological father was a pediatric surgeon. Also, her mother was a corporate estate lawyer, her sister was working on a doctorate in engineering, and her younger brother was in his first year of college. Large amounts of money were inherited on both the maternal and paternal sides. Jackson and Crystal Richmond were well-known and well-respected in their career fields and in their charitable and philanthropic activities.

Mibs mumbled to herself, "Well if I'm finding out that I have relatives I've never known about, I'm glad they are good people." She crossed her arms against her chest and thought of her aunt. "Aunt Bernie has never had large sums of money to give away, but she's been generous in so many other ways for many, many years." Mibs walked over to the small alcove that served as her bedroom and knelt down in front of the picture of Jesus, the *Divine Mercy*. "Thank you, Lord, for letting me have Bernice Monahan as a role model all these years. Please guide me as I get to know this new family. Show me how to love them, too." Gazing at the painting of Christ, she said, "Jesus, I trust in You."

Chapter 21

Jace's assistant was perplexed by her boss's request. "I guess you better explain that order a little more clearly. What lady and what dog?"

Jace instructed her to pull up a map covering Albert Borne's neighborhood. "I want the name of the woman who lives behind Borne's house. Here. Across the back alley." He pointed. "Does she live alone? What kind of dog does she have? I'm fixin' to go pay her a visit."

By the time they had stopped at the bakery and Jace had climbed back into Juan's Jeep Wrangler with two small bags in his hand, Carla had texted the requested information.

The text noted that 'the neighbor lady is Harriet Webster, widow, seventy-four years old, a retired librarian. She owns a Boston Terrier, dog's name unknown.' Jace thought about the best way to approach Mrs. Webster.

"So, you think this neighbor lady saw something?" Juan queried.

Jace shrugged. "Maybe. Maybe not. I'm thinking that it's possible Officer Nugent heard Borne reentering his back door. If that's what the noise was, then, yes, I think Harriet Webster may have seen our suspect in his backyard."

Juan furrowed his eyebrows as he glanced at Jace. "If she did, why wouldn't she say something?"

"Maybe," Jace reasoned, "no one bothered to ask her."

Jace knocked on the door of the well-maintained Cape Cod. Shuffling feet could be heard approaching the entrance. A chain lock jiggled before the door was opened six inches, stopping with the restraints of the chain. White, tightly curled hair and one brown eye could be seen through the small opening.

"Who are you? What do you want?" a sharp, raspy voice challenged.

Holding his identification close so it could be easily seen, Jace calmly introduced himself. "Detective Lieutenant Jace Trueblood, ma'am." He nodded toward Juan. "This is Detective Juan Mendoza. May we come in, Mrs. Webster?"

"Why?"

"Because I believe you and your little Boston Terrier may be of some help in our murder investigation."

"Murder?"

He let the word *murder* sink in. The older woman took time to study Jace, as well as the slightly shorter, muscular man waiting behind him. She then shut the door and unhooked the chain.

She reopened the door, swung it wide, turned without saying anything further, and allowed the two lawmen to follow her down a short hallway.

When they reached a small, tidy living room, Harriet Webster scowled at Jace. "Well, what do you want to know?"

Despite the puckered mouth that presented a sour-lipped attitude, Jace perceived that the facade didn't reach her eyes. Turning away from the grumpy woman, he knelt down in front of the small dog. Jace opened one of the bags in his left hand, pulled out a cookie, and held the dog treat near its nose. A yelp of delight escaped the black and white terrier just before the pup snatched the cookie. Then, turning twice before trotting away a few feet, the dog began chomping.

"Do you think bringing a treat for my dog is supposed to soften me up?"

"No, ma'am." Jace held out the second bag. "But I'm hopin' maybe *this* will."

Lifting her chin, Harriet Webster peered at the smiling detective. Then, slowly shifting her attention from his face to the small, white paper bag, she reached out and accepted the package. She opened the top and peeked in. Harriet tilted her head and mumbled, "Hmmm."

"I hope you like cinnamon rolls. I almost picked out muffins, but I guessed that y'all might be a cinnamon roll type of lady."

The fluffy-topped slippers flipped against her heels as she carried the bag through an arched doorway, opened a bread box, and secured the rolls inside. When she shuffled back to the living room, Harriet addressed Jace, "I wondered if anyone was going to get around to talking to me."

"Well, I *am*. Ma'am, can y'all tell us if you saw anything you think a detective like me might wanna know?"

"It seemed like the police were searching for something across the alley. I suppose somebody, like you, might want to check under those flower pots by the back porch."

Jace held another dog cookie out to the puppy. "What's his name?"

A genuine smile crossed the old woman's face when she focused on the dog. "That's Bumper. He was pretty young when I got him. Every time he tried to run, he'd bump into something and tumble over."

"That's a great name." Jace knelt down and rubbed Bumper on the head before standing and turning his eyes back to Mrs. Webster. "Ma'am, will you be good enough to take a ride down to the police station and give an official report on exactly what you saw at Albert Borne's house yesterday?"

"Do I have to go in the vehicle I saw pull up outside, or do I get a ride in a real police car?" She squinted at Jace.

"I'll have a squad car come over to give you a ride." In a quiet, almost conspiratorial tone, Jace whispered, "They can even flash the lights and hit the siren if you like."

Jace left the Webster house and walked across the alley while Juan pulled his vehicle around the block and parked. Jace proceeded to the backyard of Borne's property and motioned to a uniformed officer standing guard by the back door. He asked him to send the crime scene photographer outside. Jace marched up to a row of flower pots filled with red and pink geraniums, then looped his thumbs in his side pants pockets, scrutinizing the area as he waited for CSI photographer Samuel Portman.

A row of six large clay pots was lined up beside the porch. Each flower pot had been placed on top of a similar container, turned upside down. The rims of the upturned plant holders were sunk several inches into the ground; grass had grown around the edges of each.

"Detective Lieutenant Trueblood, what do you need?" The crime scene photographer ambled across the lawn, finding Jace studying the bright-colored geraniums.

"Get ready to snap pictures, Samuel. It's time to find evidence."

"I'm sure the team checked all around these flowers. They even checked in each planter to make sure it only had a flower and dirt in it."

"What about underneath?"

Samuel gestured toward the bottom row of large terra cotta pots. "They're buried in the ground. Since the robbery detectives got back here within a couple minutes, Borne wouldn't have had time to dig them up and rebury them," he reasoned.

"Maybe he didn't need to dig them up."

Slipping on gloves, Jace lifted the first clay container off the lower row. He nudged the lower pot with his shoe. It didn't budge, solidly settled into the ground. The second one gave the same result. However, when he tried the third one in the row, the red terra cotta pot shifted. Jace reached down and tilted the pot, slipped his fingers under the rim, and lifted.

Samuel Portman gasped at what was there and started taking photos.

Jace waited until the photographer had a snapshot from every angle before picking up the pair of size 11 men's shoes. As the shoes were raised, a clinking noise was heard. Jace reached into one of the shoes and pulled out an antique brooch.

"Benson!" Jace bellowed. His strong voice resounded through the air.

Todd Benson called back, "I'm coming. You don't have to yell." Benson joined Portman and Trueblood. The surprise in his eyes indicated that he recognized the pair of shoes the team had been actively searching for. Setting a hard-sided plastic box on the grass, Benson opened it and removed a large evidence bag. "I'm assuming you want priority processing on this evidence." He glanced at Jace, who gave him a sharp nod as he placed the shoes into the bag.

"As soon as possible, Todd. Please." Jace held out the piece of jewelry. "Put this into evidence, too."

Jace watched as the CSI group packed up, taking the critical evidence back to the lab. Then, he instructed the officer in charge at the scene to lock the place up before thanking and dismissing the team.

Jace glanced toward the neighbor's house. He started chuckling when he noticed Mrs. Webster heading to the police cruiser parked along the curb, its lights flashing.

Harriet Webster had changed into what Jace's grandmother would have called 'Sunday best' clothes. The white-haired senior had exchanged the house dress and slippers for a calf-length flowered dress and black, patten leather shoes.

She held a medium-sized black purse clutched in her hand. Her head was held high as the uniformed police officer welcomed her into the back seat of the vehicle.

The policeman happened to glance toward Jace. Recognizing the Chief of Detectives, he lifted his hand in greeting.

Jace nodded back.

Smiling, the officer gave a thumbs up, climbed in the cruiser, and hit the siren as they pulled away from the curb.

Juan had pulled his Jeep down the alley and stopped next to Jace. Rolling down the window, he shook his head. "Giving her the full effect?"

"Hey, she was a big help. Might as well let her have a little fun." Jace maneuvered around the front of the vehicle and climbed in, still chuckling.

~~

Jace watched as Borne's lawyer, Rita Yates, sat quietly, her face stony as Juan placed photos across the old, scarred table in the interrogation room.

"As you can see, Mr. Borne, these pictures were taken in *your* backyard. Under *your* flower pot, where we found a pair of brown oxford shoes." Juan pushed the photos closer.

Borne's usual unconcerned guise slowly faded. Jace noticed a hint of surprise and definite signs of disbelief across the narcissistic killer's face. "I think we all know that your DNA will be on these shoes. And I'll be astonished if we don't find traces of Mr. Patterson's blood on them."

"I'd like to consult with my client," Ms. Yates said.

Borne sat back, trying to present an air of indifference. However, the uneven legs rocked the chair slightly, causing the arrogant criminal to grit his teeth in frustration.

Jace and Juan pushed their chairs back and stepped out of the room as Yates leaned over and whispered to Borne.

It would be at least tomorrow before the lab report on the shoes was back. Jace asked Juan to make sure the suspect was secure before leaving. He then headed back to his office, directing all but the scheduled crew to leave for the rest of the day. He planned on doing the same.

Jace had been so busy working on the Patterson case that he hadn't spent as much time as he'd have liked with Mibs. Nor had he been able to help his dad and uncle with the downstairs bedroom and bathroom remodel. Although Jace wanted to join them, he knew that the two brothers could manage fine without him. He was more concerned about Mibs.

His fiancée was going through a confusing and challenging time. The DNA tests, the visit from Agent Dasher and PI Gage, and the idea of previously unknown family members had to be causing her anxiety. Wanting to brighten his sweetheart's troubled thoughts, he decided to stop at Bicker's Florist Shop and pick up some flowers.

Chapter 22

Mibs knew that Aunt Bernie's guests would be gone by now, so she had headed downstairs around 3:00, finding Bernie gathering the pinochle cards and then sliding them into the card box. Her aunt would need a nap by now, so she insisted that the dear woman go rest. After Aunt Bernie went to her room, Mibs cleaned up what little mess there was. It only took a few minutes to put things right.

She grabbed an orange ball and a blue Frisbee, and she headed for the back door. Mibs smiled when Shadow's tail wagged as soon as she'd picked up the toys. After tossing the ball several times, she switched and threw the bright-colored disk. Twenty minutes later, the girl and dog returned inside. Mibs settled back on the couch in the break room. Shadow made her way into Bernie's room, probably curled up and about to take a nap beside her mistress' bed. Mentally weary, Mibs leaned back and closed her eyes, thoughts swirling through her mind.

Half awake, half asleep, Mibs had a jumbled dream. *Faceless kidnappers chased her as she ran through a field with brightly colored swaths of cloth swirling through the air. Grabbing things that suddenly seemed to materialize around her, she threw them at the pursuing kidnappers – pincushion, patterns, measuring tapes, zippers, buttons – as she ran and ran. Finally, collapsing to the ground, she watched in horror as large hands reached toward her.*

Suddenly, she heard voices singing, 'Clara, Clara, where are you?' People began to dance around her, cutting the kidnappers off. She watched the blurred dancers as their features cleared. She recognized the faces from the folder Tony had given her – Camilla, Crystal and Jackson Richmond, and Lawrence. Aunt Bernie, Tony, and Whitney were there, too. They were all trying to protect her from the criminals. Then, she heard another voice, clearer than the others. 'Mibs, sweetheart, are you okay?' Jace was there, gently running his hand along the side of her face.

Slowly opening her eyes as she pressed her cheek into the firm but gentle hand, Mibs blinked as she separated the dream from reality. "Jace, you *are* here."

~~

"You were mumbling in your sleep. You seemed upset." Jace reached for her hands and held them as he studied her face. "It was just a dream. You're safe."

Mibs sighed. "Thank you for being here."

Jace gazed at the beautiful green eyes, slowly dropped Mibs' hands, reached for her shoulders, and pulled her into his arms. He ran a line of kisses gently down her neck before he took a breath. "I love you, Mibs."

"I love you, too," Mibs murmured, butterflies filling her stomach as she reacted to his tender kisses.

Taking a deep breath and slowly letting it out, he sat back and offered his hand. "I brought something for you."

As she accepted his hand and stood, Mibs saw

the flowers sitting on the small table. "Oh, how pretty!"

"The florist had cards that told the meaning of flowers. I picked these because they made me think of you." He lifted a card from a vase of daisies. "The daisy has several different meanings, including innocence and cheerfulness. But I chose it for true love, new beginnings, and patience." He pulled a single daisy out, broke off part of the stem, and then slipped the flower into Mibs' hair. "You are my true love. We are planning a new beginning together. And you definitely need patience at times to put up with me and my job."

"They're beautiful. I love them."

The couple turned when they heard the tap, tap, tap of Bernie's cane as she made her way down the short hall leading from her bedroom. Before Bernie came into sight, Shadow padded in and hurried over for a greeting.

Mibs gave Jace a feather-soft kiss on the cheek before bending down to rub the loyal canine between the ears.

"I thought I heard voices," the cheery aunt said. "Hello, Jace."

"Hi, Bernie." Reaching into his pocket, Jace pulled out a small bag and handed it to her. "I have something for you."

Bernie opened the bag and found a red-colored flower pin. "It's a carnation brooch."

"Yes, ma'am. According to what I read, the red carnation signifies admiration. And I certainly have a lot of admiration for you."

Bernie removed the pin from the card and attached it to the front of her blouse. "Thank you, Jace. I'll enjoy wearing this."

"I'm glad you like it."

Bernie glanced at the table. "I see you're spoiling Mibs with flowers."

"Aren't they beautiful?" Mibs beamed as she brought the description cards over to her aunt. "This explains the meaning behind the flower. The words make them extra special."

"I have read that types and colors of flowers have special significance." Aunt Bernie seemed pleased, nodding as she read the information.

"These daisies are going up to my room." Turning to Jace, Mibs said, "Thank you, honey. I think I needed these flowers today."

"Mibs, you appear to have a lot on your mind." He placed his forehead on hers. "Do you want to talk? Maybe if it isn't too cool outside for you, we could take a walk."

She nodded. "Yes, let's talk as we walk."

"Do you have a jacket handy?"

"You're dressed up. Let me run upstairs and get something a little nicer than my jacket," she said while picking up the vase of daisies. "I'll take these with me."

~~

Jace watched Mibs until she was no longer in sight.

As they waited for her niece's return, Bernie asked Jace if they'd made progress on the Patterson murder. She gave an audible sigh of relief when Jace told her they had the presumed murderer under lock and key.

"I'll wait until we get all the reports back from the crime lab, but I'm confident that we'll be able to convict the museum employee, Albert

Borne, of not only burglary and theft but also murder," Jace explained.

"Does that mean you'll be able to work more regular hours? At least for a while?"

Jace shrugged and wrinkled his brow. "I hope so. The only other major thing we have on the schedule at this time is catching the person who's been selling fake IDs to the teens in town."

"Fake identifications?" Bernie asked. "Mibs said something about that. I believe she talked to that private investigator, Macey Buckmore."

"Yes. Macey is working on things with a couple of officers from the station." Jace rubbed the back of his neck. "I don't want a young person or anyone hurt again by someone driving under the influence."

~~

"Ready?" Mibs had returned wearing a sky-blue, knee-length coat with a fluffy white collar. Navy gloves covered her hands, and a navy, felt cloche hat fit stylishly on her head. The bell-shaped cap had one edge of the brim turned down, and a velvet bow decorated the other side.

"Yep, I'm ready." Jace's face brightened as his eyes ran over her. "You sure are purdy'."

"Thank you." Mibs slipped her hand through his arm.

"Oh, Bernie," Jace stopped to ask, "would you like to go out for dinner? I'd like to take you and Mibs out tonight."

"That sounds nice. Did you have anywhere specific in mind?"

"Well, Mibs and I have gone to *Mes Amis* a few times."

Jace asked Bernie, "Have you been to that restaurant?"

"I have not, but I think I would enjoy eating there. But maybe we can go early. I do tend to get tired later in the evening."

"No problem, Bernie." Jace checked his watch. "Why don't we leave around 5:30? That gives Mibs and me time for our walk first."

"Good. I'll go change. It will be fun to dress up a little."

~~

Mibs and Jace strolled down the street arm in arm. The cool November breeze ruffled the girl's soft tresses, which peeked out of her hat, and brought a rosy glow to her cheeks. Jace ignored the breath of wind, his eyes fixed on his girl. For a few minutes, the couple was lost in the autumn ambiance, wrapped in the simple joy of each other's company. When they reached the small park in the center of town, they stepped into the octagonal-shaped, open-sided pavilion. They approached one of the wooden benches, and they snuggled, sharing warmth.

After a few minutes of silence, Mibs began to speak. "I met my sister today."

Jace sat up straighter. "You met Camilla?"

"Yes. She came by the shop."

"Okay," Jace muttered. "Are you all right? Was it a good..." He wasn't quite sure how to ask. "...or not-so-good meeting?"

She gazed into Jace's eyes. "It was good. As soon as we saw each other, we...well, it was like we already knew each other. I don't know how to explain it. All these years, I never knew I had a twin. But when we saw each other, there was an indescribable connection. Like..." Mibs paused and shrugged. "There was a part of me in her and a part of her in me."

Jace sat quietly, holding her hand, letting her thoughts settle. Then, after a few minutes of silence, he asked, "Mibs, are you glad that you've learned the truth about your...your heritage?"

"At first, I was just confused. Then, I became mad." Leaning her head against Jace's shoulder, Mibs curled her hand around the soft lapel of his overcoat. "Then, I asked myself, 'Who am I mad at?' Certainly not my biological parents. Maybe the kidnappers? After a while, I decided that getting upset wouldn't change things. Now...." She lifted her head and gazed into his concerned eyes. "Now, I think I'm glad. I can't imagine the anguish Crystal and Jackson Richmond have gone through all these years. At least that terrible uncertainly is gone." She sat back and crossed her arms, and then Mibs gave a sharp, affirmative nod. "I always wanted a brother or sister. Now I have both. I have a newfound family. I'm beginning to like the idea."

Watching the resolute attitude that he had learned to admire return to his girl's demeanor, Jace smiled at the determined set of her chin and the unflinching glint in her eyes. "Good." Jace sat back and crossed his arms in imitation of her fixed posture.

It took only a moment for her to realize he was teasing her and trying to make her laugh by copying her attitude. Mibs shook her head as she smiled. "Jace Trueblood, you are good, not just to me, but *for* me. You help keep my life in balance."

Jace gave her a fake frown and sighed. "Well, you don't keep me very balanced. Whenever I'm around you, my head starts spinning, and my heart beats faster. Woman, you turn my world all cattywampus."

Mibs couldn't help giggling. "Catty...what?"

Jace reached over and pulled her into his arms. "Darlin', let's just say that I can't think straight when you get close to me."

Mibs reached up and ran her hands through his hair. "And you, my southern gentleman, make me feel things I've never felt before." She gave him a long, passionate kiss before leaning away.

No more words were spoken as they gazed into each other's eyes. Then, the quiet moment was suddenly interrupted by a cacophony of shouts and laughter from a large group of teens in the park. From the footballs they carried and the good-natured conversations floating back and forth, it was apparent that an impromptu football game was about to begin.

"I guess we'd better head back. I should take Shadow outside for a few minutes before we leave for dinner. Which reminds me," Jace said as he pulled his cell phone out. "I'll call *Mes Amis* and ask them to keep a table for three for around 5:45."

"Oh! Maybe you can make another reservation."

"Okay." Jace tilted his head.

"I told Camilla that I'd talk to you and see if we could set a time for us to meet her parents...ah, my parents. She said they would come here unless I wanted to go to Metrofield."

The noise from the rambunctious young adults grew louder. Jace stood, pulled Mibs up with him, and searched his phone for the number for the *Mes Amis* restaurant as they began strolling away from the center of town.

"Did she say how soon they want to come to Havendale?" Jace asked.

"She gave the impression that soon would be best. She's waiting at the Holiday Inn."

"Here in Havendale? She's still here?"

Mibs nodded. "She decided not to make the long drive back to Metrofield today. I'm supposed to call her after talking to you."

"Okay. Call Camilla. See if there's any way they can come within the next few days. Ask if it will be just Mr. and Mrs. Richmond, or would she and their son, Lawrence, be there, too."

Mibs reached into her pocket and pulled out the paper she'd written Camilla's phone number on. As she began punching in the number, Jace interrupted.

"If your sister is still in town, maybe she'd like to join us for our early dinner this evening."

"I'll ask her."

~~

When they got back to the shop, Aunt Bernie was waiting for them. She'd change to a deep, burgundy-colored collarless jacket and matching skirt. She'd pinned her new carnation brooch to the upper left front of the jacket. Her pure white hair and the white ruffled silk blouse peeking out of the jacket's neckline gave a noticeable contrast to the rich color of the suit.

"Aunt Bernie, your outfit is very nice," Jace declared.

Eyes twinkling at the compliment, Bernie gave an accepting nod. "Thank you, Jace. It's been a while since I've dressed up for dinner at a fancy restaurant."

"That suit is fabulous, Aunt Bernie," Mibs agreed. "By the way, I hope you don't mind if we go out to eat twice this week. Camilla talked to her parents. They're going to meet us at 6:30 Wednesday evening."

A flicker of surprise crossed Bernie's face. It was quickly replaced by a calm expression of acceptance. "I'll be ready."

Covering her mouth with her hand, Mibs stammered, "Oh, Aunt Bernie, I should have asked you first."

"Ask me what? Do you mean about meeting the Richmonds?"

Mibs reached out, placing her hand on her aunt's arm. "I'm talking about today. I told Jace that Camilla was still in Havendale. He suggested that we invite her to join us at the restaurant." Mibs asked, "Do you mind if she has dinner with us tonight?"

"Of course, I don't mind." Bernie smiled. "I want to get to know the whole bunch of them. I want to learn about anyone who's going to be part of your life."

Mibs gave her aunt a hug. Then, Mibs unbuttoned her coat, showing the dress slacks and honey-colored cashmere sweater, which she'd changed into when she went upstairs earlier. "Do you two think this outfit is okay for the restaurant? Or should I change to a dress?"

"I think your outfit is perfect," Aunt Bernie said.

"I wouldn't change a thing." There was genuine appreciation in Jace's eyes.

Chapter 23

Monday morning's temperature rose unexpectedly by ten degrees, not a significant change but enough to be appreciated. Jace pulled up behind Monahan's Sewing Shop and let Shadow follow him out of the driver's side before shutting the door. The duo headed toward the back entrance. Suddenly, a squirrel darted across the grass-covered strip at the end of the parking lot. Shadow watched the bristly-tailed animal scramble up a small tree. The dog's body quivered with the inborn desire to chase the racing critter, stymied by her training as a military canine.

Jace bent down and rubbed the dog's head. "Girl, you're retired now. You're no longer on active duty. So, go be a regular dog. Run and chase that old squirrel if you want." Jace gave a gesture and said, "Go get 'im."

Shadow looked at Jace as if to ask – 'is it really okay?' before shooting across the lawn, barking as she circled the tree.

The shop's back door opened. Mibs stepped outside, shrugging into her jacket.

"Are you two having fun?" Mibs shook her head, "because I don't think the squirrel is."

Jace whistled to Shadow. When she froze and turned toward him, he said, "Come here, girl. I think that varmint has had enough for now."

Obediently, the well-trained canine headed back and stood expectantly by his side. As

Shadow panted with her tongue hanging out, she wagged her tail when Jace leaned down and rubbed her head.

"You're a good dog, Shadow. Yes, you are." Glancing up, Jace noticed that Mibs watched them, a questioning expression on her face. "Oh, don't worry, Mibs. There's nothing wrong with a dog chasing a squirrel. It's about time Shadow's allowed to be a normal dog."

Jace straightened and sauntered over to his girl. Mibs wore a daisy in her hair, one from the bouquet he'd given her, and it warmed his heart. He tilted his head toward Shadow before saying, "The first dog I ever had was an old Treeing Walker coonhound. I got Bugle one summer when I visited my Uncle Jack's farm. I gave him that name 'cause he sounded just like a bugle when he treed a raccoon and gave out a bay. About four years later, my uncle was happy he'd given me that hound. During the summer I turned thirteen, a bobcat was roaming the local farms and killing sheep and chickens. Usually, those cats avoid areas where humans are, but I reckon that old lynx had gotten a taste for sheep. The neighbors were all fit to be tied, so they got together to track it down. Bugle and I happened to be there that summer. Bugle was the one who found the right trail and treed that big cat, alerting us all with a shrill howl."

"Did the bobcat end up being killed?"

Jace knew that Mibs understood the necessity of ending this animal's reign of terror on the local livestock but hated the need for it to die. "No, darlin', we didn't kill it. One of the more experienced hunters slipped some kind of pole with a coil loop at the end over its head. He managed to get the bobcat caged and sent to a specified mountain area in another county."

Jace put his arm around Mibs and guided her back to the store. "I've known a lot of farmers, ranchers, and hunters over the years. I know that they are some of the most conservation-minded people in the country. They love the land, the trees, and the wildlife. They seem to understand that God made us stewards of the earth and its plants and animals. But, He also gave us the use of those same things to fill human needs for food, survival, and the enjoyment that nature's beauty provides. We just need to remember to use what we need, leave what we don't need in peace, and replace what we can."

"Hmm. That's good to know." Mibs gave an accepting nod. She glanced at the dog. "Shadow, I guess it's okay if you play tag with that squirrel. I just hope you don't catch him."

Jace chuckled, then tipped her head up, leaned down, and kissed her lips. "I've got to get to work. Have a good day, sweetheart. Enjoy your time with Camilla." As he was about to pull the door closed, he said, "I like your sister. I'm glad you two found each other."

After the pleasant dinner at the restaurant the previous night, Mibs and Camilla had made plans to spend several hours together today. Jace knew that Mibs wanted to show her sister around Havendale and have lunch at the Blueberry Grove Café. He hoped they would have quality time to talk and make memories.

This afternoon, Camilla planned to drive home to Metrofield. Then, fly back with her family on Wednesday to meet Mibs, Jace, and Bernie at *Mes Amis* in the evening.

~~

Jace had been at his desk going through messages and emails for almost an hour when Todd Benson entered the office.

He pulled his eyes away from the computer and the taxing email he'd been trying to compose and greeted Benson. "Hey, Todd. Come on in."

Benson placed a file on the lieutenant's desk and, sliding it forward, Benson said, "We worked most of the night to get these results, so... you owe me."

Jace picked up the file, scanning the contents quickly. One side of his mouth quirked up, gratified with the report. He returned to the beginning and reread the information more slowly the second time. Then, peering up at the crime scene specialist, he said, "Good work, Todd. I do owe you." Wrinkling his brow, he asked, "A good dinner, tickets to a game? What'll it be?"

"An extra day off," Benson responded without hesitation. "For my crew and me."

"I'll clear it with personnel."

As Benson turned and headed out the door, Jace picked up the phone and called Captain Taylor.

"Hank, we got him. Do you want to join me at the interrogation room in about forty minutes?"

After receiving an affirmative response, Jace called the lawyer, Rita Yates.

Jace and Captain Taylor reached the small eight-by-twelve feet area. This room carried out the dual task as an interview place for those making a statement or being informed about something and an interrogation room for more strenuous discussion with a suspected criminal. He peeked through the small square window in the room's door. Rita Yates was already sitting at the table, having what appeared to be a heated discussion with her client.

Borne and Yates turned toward the entrance when the handle clicked, and the door swished open. The lawyer sat back, placing her hands flat on the table. The accused criminal squared his shoulders and folded his arms across his chest. The arrogant art handler jutted his chin forward, daring the lawmen to challenge him.

Neither Jace nor Hank sat down, standing in front of the table. Both men towered over the suspect and his lawyer. Jace opened the folder and took his time paging through the sheets of information, letting Borne stew in the silence of the room. Finally, Jace pulled out a picture, placing it between Borne and Yates.

"So?" Borne sniggered. "What does this prove?"

"Do you see the discoloration in the treads of this shoe?" No answer to the rhetorical question was expected. "That's blood. To be precise, that's Roger Patterson's blood. And the DNA evidence on the shoe is proof that this loafer belongs to you." Jace tapped the picture exhibited in front of Borne.

"Albert Borne," Captain Taylor spoke. "You are under arrest for burglary, theft, and felony first-degree murder."

"Can we talk about a deal?" Rita Yates glanced back and forth between Trueblood and Taylor.

"I can't think of anything that would make us want to make a deal." Taylor shook his head.

Yates leaned over and whispered to her client. She waited for him to respond. Finally, he nodded, still glaring at Lieutenant Trueblood with disdain.

"What if my client can tell you where some of the missing pieces from the museum were sold? Could we lower the first-degree murder charge?"

Captain Taylor stepped closer to Jace and whispered. Jace didn't move his eyes away from Borne as he decisively shook his head.

"We found the brooch you stole the other day. The pieces you took in the past could be anywhere by now." Jace cut his eyes over to the captain. "I'll rely on our robbery department to track them down–if that's even possible."

Shaking his head at Borne, Hank said, "No deal." He stepped over and opened the door, motioning in two police officers. As soon as they had Albert Borne in handcuffs, the captain left the room.

Jace followed him out. When they were down the hall, Jace said, "I'm sure that the museum would like to get some of those antiques back, but I don't think that murderer deserves any kind of deal."

"Oh, I agree with you, Jace." Taylor rubbed

the back of his neck as he stared at Jace. "Do you think our robbery and fraud division will come up with anything?"

"I hope so. Officers Nugent and Iverson were seeking out some of the fences they'd dealt with in the past. I'll call them tomorrow and see if they've come up with anything." Stopping next to the break room, Jace stepped through the doorway. "I'm getting a coffee. How 'bout y'all, Hank?"

"I've had my limit of caffeine for the day." Hank slapped Jace on the back. "Good job at closing this murder case."

"It was a lot of teamwork, boss. We've got some good people working here."

"We do. But, the team wouldn't be as efficient if it didn't have a good leader directing them." Captain Taylor nodded. "I mean that, Jace."

"Thanks, Captain." Jace ran his hand across his chin, feeling the compliment was unnecessary. He was just doing his job.

"How is the situation with the phony IDs going? Any progress?"

"Detective Clearwater and the others are heading back to the bus station after two o'clock, so they'll be there before school lets out today. We don't know which days the forger does business. Hopefully, he hasn't caught on to the fact that we're keeping the place under surveillance. If we don't get any results by Friday evening, we may develop a different plan. I want to catch this guy in the act. He needs to be charged with a felony crime. Because of the injuries and death of those teens, I hope he doesn't get off with a slap on the wrist."

"Some people don't think of the permanent damage their actions can cause." Taylor shook his head, then turned and made his way down the hall.

Chapter 24

Eve poured a few peanuts into her hand, then handed the small bag to Martha Schroeder. Eve smiled at the policewoman who'd been waiting with her for the past two hours. "Getting bored, Martha?"

"Nah," the tall brunette dressed in civilian clothes responded. "I don't mind 'people watching.' Besides, this is better than being cooped up in a car on a stakeout."

Thinking about the time before she became a detective and had spent many hours in a patrol car, Eve had to agree with that comment. She was about to mention one particular tedious surveillance job when she saw a man approaching the building. He fit the general description of the person they were watching for.

"Look sharp, Schroeder. We might have a live one coming in."

They watched the guy enter through the revolving door. He was a young man wearing a hooded sweatshirt. He cautiously scanned the large entrance room of the bus station and let his eyes shift around. Eve realized that he was studying the occupants of the lobby.

A stout man wearing dark navy blue coveralls pushed a shop broom across the floor; the maintenance man seemed bored, apparently not paying attention to the foot traffic drifting through the bus station. Eve hoped that the hooded individual glancing at her and

Schroeder saw two ladies with shopping bags nestling around them, sharing an animated conversation. His eyes skimmed over a couple with a toddler. They were at the ticket window, apparently checking the train schedule. Two teen boys, leaning against a far wall, saw the man who'd just entered, but they quickly turned away.

The guy, seemingly satisfied that there was no threat awaiting him, sauntered over to locker number 57. As soon as he slipped the key in, the two teens scurried over and whispered to him. The shorter of the two boys pulled something out of his pocket and handed it to the owner of locker 57. Turning slightly, the young, hooded man snatched the money from the teen and then pulled an item from the locker, slapping it into the boy's hand.

Since the hooded guy was focused on the transaction, he hadn't seen the maintenance man give a decisive nod to Eve and Martha. He didn't notice that the ladies were no longer sitting on the wooden bench but had moved up to within a few feet of him and the teens.

"Gentlemen," Eve held out her badge as she addressed the trio. "I'm Detective Clearwater, and this is Officer Schroeder. I need you to face the lockers and put your hands against the wall."

Stunned, the two teens froze. After a couple of seconds, one boy gulped loudly, and the other started to shake, but they both complied with the order. However, the slightly older man slammed the locker shut and turned to run.

The forger got less than four feet before falling

flat on his face. The maintenance man had pushed the long-handle broom across the guy's escape route, causing him to trip. As Martha Schroeder leaned down and clicked a pair of handcuffs on the felon's wrists, Macey Buckmore smiled. "I surely don't think you're going anywhere except to jail." A broad grin lit up Macey's face as he picked up his broom.

"You're under arrest for felony possession and sale of fake identifications." Schroeder recited the Miranda warning as she helped the hooded young man to his feet.

"I don't know what you're talking about," he squawked. "If those boys have fake IDs, they didn't get them from me."

"Sorry, but that won't wash. I'm wearing a body camera, and we've recorded the whole transaction." Officer Schroeder moved aside the scarf, revealing the camera. Realizing that he'd been caught, the forger clamped his mouth shut.

Detective Clearwater motioned the two teens to move to the door. Even though the boys would probably only receive a small fine and probation, she hoped they would learn a valuable lesson. She'd rather have them scared about going to the police station and embarrassed about having to call their parents than face other possible complications from underage drinking and driving.

By early evening, the fake ID forger was processed and under lock and key. The two sixteen-year-old students had been released into the custody of their parents and would be showing up to talk to a judge in the near future.

Eve was behind her desk finishing up a report, Officer Martha Schroeder and Macey Buckmore occupying two chairs in front of her. She'd asked the two to wait until she finished her statement because she wanted to treat them to dinner. Glancing up, Eve noted the calm expression on Martha's face. Macey, however, appeared to be beaming with pride from his part on the surveillance team.

"Good job, team." Lieutenant Trueblood stopped to congratulate them on the successful outcome.

Eve turned to face the lead detective and nodded toward Schroeder and Buckmore. "Having help from these two made the task easier."

"Thanks for your assistance, Officer Schroeder." Jace shook Martha's hand, then Macey's.

Pulling an envelope out of his pocket, he handed it to the private detective. "Here you go, Mr. Buckmore. The captain already okayed a check for your services. He listed it as a consulting fee."

"Anytime! Anytime!" Macey beamed.

Eve shut down her computer and stood. "We're going out to eat. Would you like to join us?" she asked Jace.

"Thanks, but no. I'm picking up Mibs and her aunt. They're coming over to my house, so Aunt Bernie can give me her opinion on the bedroom and bath that has been remodeled for her."

"Mibs' aunt will be living with you two after you're married?" Eve had wondered about the aged woman living by herself.

Jace nodded. "Oh, yeah. Bernie is a feisty old lady, but she's a little unsteady on her feet at times. There'll be less worrying if Mibs and I know she's sleeping on the first floor of our home instead of in a building several streets away. I plan on hooking up a system, so she can buzz upstairs if she needs something and can't get to her phone."

"Sounds good," Eve said. She pulled open her desk drawer and retrieved her purse. "See you tomorrow, Lieutenant."

Chapter 25

"This is wonderful, Jace." Bernice ran her hand across the beautiful, straight grain of the cocoa-colored walnut paneling featured on one wall. The other walls of the bedroom were painted a pale, buttercup yellow. The previously small window had been replaced with a large bay window, a cushioned bench nestled beneath. The curtains framing the window were made from smooth, lustrous brocade, and matching material covered the bench.

Leaning on her cane as she made her way over to the bed, Bernice fingered the delicate embroidery stitches decorating the edge of a bright-white pillowcase. She knew that Mibs had been working on a set of pillowcases in the evenings, but her niece had refused to let her see them before they were done.

"These are beautiful, Mibs. Thank you." Bernice smiled as she focused on the depiction of butterflies in a field of buttercups sewn into the fabric at the edge of each pillow slip. One of her favorite quilts covered the bed. The *Grandma's Flower Garden* quilt featured the room's yellow and cocoa color theme. Burnt orange and garnet shades scattered through the quilt gave a nice color contrast.

"Check out the updated bathroom, Aunt Bernie," Mibs suggested.

When she stepped into the handicap-equipped room, Bernice stared in amazement. This room was twice the size of her old bathroom. Even if she ended up in a wheelchair, there would be room to maneuver. Blue-and-white tiles glistened above the sink and counter. The large walk-in shower had a built-in bench and several grab bars within easy reach. Jace had knocked out the back wall, stealing room from the laundry area. But she had no idea that it would enlarge the bathroom this much.

Bernice felt herself sigh contentedly as she took in the remodeled room. It had only been a few years since she'd made the major move from the two-story house she'd lived in for over twenty years to the bedroom at the back of Monahan's. Moving again hadn't seemed all that appealing. However, this comfortably furnished bedroom and bath had Bernie thinking that the move might not be so bad.

She'd had doubts about moving into the house that would be Mibs and Jace's first home together. Would she be a burden? Would she be in the newlyweds' way? A few years away from ninety, Bernice didn't relish living alone. However, she would be willing to do so rather than interfere in the young couple's life.

Now that she had been reminded of how big this renovated Georgian Colonial was, she felt better. Her room was down a short hall, just past the kitchen. The rest of the bedrooms were upstairs. Mibs and Jace would have their own space, and so would she. Plus, the living room, dining room, and extensive library provided plenty of room to share.

When Bernice sighed again, Mibs slipped her hand through her arm. "Aunt Bernie, are you getting tired? Let's sit down in the dining room, and you can tell us if there is anything that you'd like changed in your rooms."

Jace brought a carton of milk from the kitchen. He poured drinks as Bernice hooked her cane on the back of the chair Mibs had pulled out. A loving smile crossed Bernice's lips as she settled into the chair at the end of the long dining room table, watching the couple puttering around the room.

"Is there anything you want me to add or change, Bernie?" Jace queried.

"I can't think of anything that would make that gorgeous bedroom and wonderful bathroom any better. Thank you for all the work you did, Jace."

"I'm glad you like it." Jace's eyes twinkled. "However, I have to give credit to my dad and uncle. They've been here doing the work and just left this afternoon on a fishing trip. They're planning on stopping back in Havendale next week to visit with us."

Mibs placed a plate of oatmeal raisin cookies on the table and grinned. "I would find it amazing that they could get the changes done so quickly, but I know they've had years of experience."

"Yep, they may be retired, but I don't know anyone who could do better work," Jace responded as he picked up the plate of cookies and moved them to a narrow buffet. "No cookies right now."

"What?" Mibs asked. "Why not?"

"Because...." Jace was interrupted by a carillon bells chime. "Someone is at the front door." Winking at Mibs, he added, "I told y'all I ordered dinner. It includes dessert, so I don't want you two spoilin' your appetites."

"I like the musical notes of the doorbell," Bernice said as it pealed again.

"Tony found that door chime in an antique store. Apparently, it was from the 1930s," Mibs explained. "He thought it would be perfect for this house. So, he gave it to us as a housewarming present."

"That was a nice gift," Bernice agreed. "And this beautiful table! This wasn't here the last time I came over." The long extending table could seat ten people easily. Four sturdy chairs lined each side of the table, and two more filled a space at each end. Bernice noticed that the buffet and the china cabinet matched the dining set.

"Jace's father, Christopher, refinished the whole set for us. He's been working on it since last summer," Mibs told Bernice. "I was told that the set is from the early 1900s, pine top over a solid oak frame and turned oak legs."

"Is this some of the furniture they found in that large garage?" Bernice asked.

"Yes, it is. And you should see the bed Chris and Jace found lying across the rafters in the back of the building. The headboard and footboard have a *fleur-de-lis* design hand-carved into the cherry wood."

"That sounds beautiful." The joy Bernice saw on her niece's face made her happy.

Jace brought the delivered food to the table. Mibs pulled dishes from the kitchen cabinet and passed them around. The dishes Jace had in his cupboard were a diverse mixture of plates, bowls, and cups which, as Jace had told them, had been left in the house by his Uncle Ezekiel.

Bernice studied the dinner plate and saw a piece of pink depression glass. The dish in front of Mibs was a luncheon plate in the Golden Wheat pattern, and Jace had been given a plate with an antique rose design.

"I haven't seen some of these dish designs for years. I'd say that some nice sets of dishes have gone through this house."

"As long as I have something to eat off of, it doesn't bother me what kind of dishes I use." Jace shrugged. "But I guess since we might want to invite guests over occasionally, a matched set would be better."

"Aunt Bernie is giving us the Blue Willow set for everyday use," Mibs reminded Jace. "And when your mom brings her set of Wedgewood China over, we'll have dishes for special occasions."

"Why don't you bring the Blue Willow over here soon?" Bernice suggested. "We can switch them out with the mixed set in your cupboard, Jace."

"Whatever you ladies want is fine with me," he responded agreeably.

As soon as Jace had spread the dinner across the table, Bernice could see why he wanted them to skip the cookies. Besides the salad and entree, there were four different kinds of desserts.

"Those are some fancy desserts." Bernice leaned over to get a better look at the sweets.

There were large squares of frosted chocolate cake decorated with pink rosebuds, golden-brown apple tarts, raspberry-topped mini cheesecakes, and what appeared to be miniature ceramic cups of *crème Brulee*.

"When I made the reservations at *Mes Amis* for Wednesday evening, I asked to speak to the owner, Raphael Pascal. I've met Mr. Pascal at city business organization meetings a few times. I told him I was meeting my fiancée's family for the first time and asked for his recommendation. Mr. Pascal enthusiastically informed me that their desserts were excellent. So, I thought we'd try some out tonight."

"I'm surprised you got a reservation for seven people on such short notice. I hear that reservations for a large group have to be made several weeks ahead." Mibs slid some baked salmon onto her plate.

Jace took the container from Mibs. "The majority of the tables in the main dining room were already reserved. Fortunately, a reservation for one of the restaurant's private rooms had been canceled. I snapped it up and had them mark us down for 6:30. By the way, I made the reservation for eight people. I called Tony and invited him too. He helped find your family, and I think he wants to meet them."

Mibs nodded. "I think that was a good idea." Dipping a serving spoon into a dish of potatoes, she asked, "What kind of potatoes do we have here?"

Jace pulled the receipt out of the delivery bag. "They're called *Potatoes Dauphinoise*. If I remember the description correctly, they are potatoes cooked with cheese, cream, and a hint of herbs. I think it was garlic, thyme, and something else I don't recall."

"Mmm." Mibs inhaled the enticing aroma. "It smells delicious."

After everyone's plate was filled, they bowed their heads and asked God to bless their meal.

Bernice added to the prayer. "Dear Lord, please bless the Richmond family, and let Your love and grace shine down as we gather together on Wednesday night."

"Amen," Mibs and Jace responded.

Shadow had been stretched out on a rug in the corner of the kitchen watching her humans enjoy their meal. When Bernice felt a nudge against her leg, she realized that the dog had moved next to her chair. She slipped a small piece of salmon to the loyal pet. When she raised her head back up, Bernice saw Jace grinning. He'd obviously caught her feeding the dog again.

"We all spoil Shadow, but I think you've become her favorite," Jace said. "Shadow usually sleeps upstairs with me when she's here and in your bedroom when she's at your place. Where do you think she will end up at night after you move in?"

Bernice shrugged, feeling a little smug as she patted the dog's head.

Chapter 26

The black Dodge Challenger pulled up to the curb in front of the house on Maple Avenue shortly before 6:00 on Wednesday evening. Tony killed the engine and grabbed the two bottles of chilled champagne he'd kept cool in a thermal container during the forty-five-minute drive. Before he reached the porch, the front door opened.

"Hi, Vitali," Jace greeted. "I heard the car as I came down the stairs."

"Hello, Trueblood." Tony handed over the Don Perignon. "You might want to put these in the fridge."

Jace glanced at the champagne. "Nice. Thanks for bringing this."

"My pleasure. I hope we'll want to celebrate and enjoy it later."

Tony got a call from Jace earlier that day, informing him of a slight addition to the planned evening. The decision had been made to see how the initial meeting with Mibs' newly discovered family went. If the gathering went well, Jace would invite the Richmonds to his house for dessert. If things seemed too tense, they would end the visit at the restaurant after dinner.

"Yep," Jace responded. "I figured Mr. and Mrs. Richmond might like to see where Mibs will be livin' after we're married. And it will give everyone a better chance to talk informally after we leave the restaurant."

Jace motioned toward the hallway. "Mibs

and Bernie are in the back."

As Tony followed Jace through the entranceway, he noticed a chandelier. "Wow, buddy. When did you put that up? That's impressive."

"Dad and I uncovered an old crate among the things stored in the garage. Findin' that chandelier when we opened the crate was about the last thing we expected. We figured it would be a major restoration job when we realized what it was. But we were surprised when we inspected it and found that it was intact. We only had to replace a couple of teardrops and prisms and put in some new sockets." Nodding with self-satisfaction, Jace said, "It sure does look mighty fine."

When Tony reached the dining room, he found Aunt Bernie sitting at the end of the table folding cloth napkins. Leaning down, he placed a kiss on the soft, wrinkled cheek. "Hello, Aunt Bernie."

"Anthony, how are you this evening?"

"I'm fine. Are you ready for tonight?"

"Yes. I am." An expression of acceptance filled her face. "This morning, I remembered a verse from St. Matthew that gave me a sense of peace. It reminds us how God takes care of the birds in the sky, so, even more, He will take care of us." She patted Tony's hand. "Things will work out the way they're supposed to."

"Hi, Tony." Mibs stepped out of the kitchen with a stack of dessert plates, placing them on the buffet. Jace had gone into the kitchen, then followed Mibs into the dining room. He carried cups and saucers from the set of Blue Willow dishes, which they'd brought over earlier that day. "I have the coffee pot set up, so we just have to push the button when we get back."

"Jace, would you and Tony grab the champagne flutes from the china cabinet, please?" Mibs asked as she picked up the napkins Bernie had folded and placed them near the dishes.

Mibs put her hands on the sides of her face, her forehead wrinkled in concentration. "Is there anything I forgot to do? Is my dress all right?"

"Sweetheart, you don't need to do anything else, and your dress is beautiful. Let's go to the restaurant before you get any more nervous." Jace placed the last glass on the buffet. He grabbed Mibs' coat from the back of a chair and held it out to her.

"Let me help you with yours, Aunt Bernie." Tony picked up the caramel-colored Burberry trench coat and assisted Bernie in putting her arms in.

"Why don't we all ride in my car?" Tony offered as they headed to the front door.

~~

The polished brass trim in the foyer glistened, light reflecting from the crystal fixtures hanging from the domed ceiling. A pair of velvet-covered settees arranged against the wall on the chiseled Travertine tiled floor presented a welcoming ambiance. Although Mibs had visited this place before, she was in awe. When Jace, Mibs, Bernie, and Tony entered the restaurant, they barely had a chance to take in their elegant surroundings before two *Mes Amis* greeters offered to take their coats.

After shedding his overcoat, Jace offered his arm to Mibs, knowing Tony would escort Bernie. Stepping up to the podium, he gave his name.

"Mr. Trueblood, we have your table ready." The friendly host made a motion with his hand, and a well-groomed man in the restaurant's uniform of black slacks, white shirt, and black and silver striped tie quickly stepped up.

They were led through the main dining area and into a room containing a large oval table surrounded by eight chairs. Sky blue linen slipcovers draped elegantly over the backs of the chairs, covered the seats, then hung gracefully to the floor. The table was set with silver-trimmed porcelain dishes and crystal glassware. A low flower arrangement of white lilies and white chrysanthemums graced the center of the table. The artistic and stylish dinner setting emphasized the elegance of the restaurant.

The prices at *Mes Amis* were considered high by Havendale standards, but appraising the prestigious surroundings and courteous and professional staff, Mibs thought it worth every penny.

They had barely sat down when a wine steward appeared, presenting a wine list to Jace.

"Tony, you know more about wines than I do. Would you order something nice for us?"

"I'd be glad to." Tony scanned the list, choosing a white wine and a red. "I don't know what foods everyone will order, so let's go with this Merlot and…" slowly, running his finger down the laminated page, he stopped near the bottom, "…I believe this French *Sauvignon Blanc* would be nice."

A waitress filled each water glass with chilled water and asked if they would like coffee, tea, or soft drinks. She had just taken their drink orders when the other expected guests arrived.

Camilla stepped into the private dining room. An older teen stood beside her. Although Lawrence had brown hair and blue eyes and was taller than his sisters, he resembled Mibs and Camilla in his facial features. Behind them, Jackson and Crystal Richmond filled the doorway.

As they entered, Mibs slowly stood. She took a jagged breath. Jace reached for her hand, holding it firmly.

When Mrs. Richmond saw Mibs, she hesitated, covering her mouth with a hand, her eyes widening. Mr. Richmond stopped by his wife, staring at the daughter he hadn't seen for twenty-four years.

Jackson Richmond placed his arm around Crystal's shoulder, guiding her forward as they followed Camilla and Lawrence to the table. Jace and Tony stood to greet the family.

Jace, acting as host, took the lead as he extended his hand to Crystal Richmond, then to Jackson. "How do you do? I'm Jace Trueblood." Lifting his hand toward Bernie, he said, "This is Bernice Monahan, Mibs' aunt." He then introduced Anthony Vitali. "And this…" Jace moved Mibs' chair back and stood behind her, placing his hands supportively on her shoulders. "...is Mirabelle Monahan. Even though you named her Clara, we know her as Mibs."

~~

Jace thought that Mr. Richmond would be the first to say something. But it was Mrs. Richmond who spoke in barely a whisper.

"Clara. My sweet Clara." Slowly stepping forward, Crystal held out her arms.

Without hesitation, Mibs closed the distance between them and embraced her biological mother. Tears of joy spilled from Crystal's eyes.

"Mibs." Camilla tapped Mibs on the arm and quietly said, "I think she needs this."

Mibs took the napkin from her sister and gently wiped away the tears from Crystal's face. Mibs said, "I'm glad you're here, Mother." Then, turning her head, she looked at Jackson Richmond. "Hello, Father. It's nice to meet you."

Jackson studied the girl in front of him and seemed to take in every detail of her face before responding. "You *are* her, aren't you? Yes! You *are* my daughter." Then, slowly shaking his head, Jackson said, "I'm sorry. I'm so sorry. I should have searched harder for you. I shouldn't have given up." His voice cracked as he said, "I didn't think you were alive, didn't think you survived the kidnapping." Slowly, raising his right hand to touch Mibs' face, he repeated, "I'm so sorry."

"Don't be sorry," Mibs responded. "I've had a good life. Aunt Bernie made sure of that." Mibs cast a loving glance at her aunt. "I want you to get to know her and see what a wonderful person she is."

Crystal Jackson smiled at Bernie. Then, stepping to the chair next to her, she asked, "May I sit here?"

"Of course," Bernie replied.

"Thank you for taking care of her." Crystal placed her hand over Bernie's. Crystal Jackson's emotion-filled blue eyes studied the knowing hazel eyes of Bernice Monahan. They began to talk.

"You must be Lawrence," Mibs, still standing next to Jackson, greeted her brother.

"Yep. That's me." Lawrence came around the table. Then, with a teasing grin, he commented, "So, does this mean I have to put up with two sisters? I can't imagine having two Camillas around."

"Hey!" Camilla retorted. "Be nice, or we might gang up on you."

"That's what I'm afraid of." A loving glint was evident in his eyes.

Uncertain but hopeful, Jace encouraged the group to sit down at the elegant table and order their food. As expected, the food was delicious. The wait staff was professional, efficient, and attentive. As the meal progressed, the extended family talked, getting to know each other. Jace kept an eye on Mibs, wanting to make sure she didn't become too overwhelmed. Mibs seemed to be taking things in stride. Jace realized that Crystal Richmond made an effort to hold her emotions in. He noticed several times when tears brimmed at the edges of her eyes, and she tilted her head down to gently wipe them dry.

The seating arrangement ended up with Mibs sitting between her parents. Jace sat on the other side of Jackson Richmond, and Bernie was next to Crystal Jackson. Tony ended up between Camilla and Lawrence and apparently took the opportunity to get to know Mibs' siblings.

"So, you are a detective on the Havendale police force; is that correct, Mr. Trueblood?" Jackson asked. "Or should I call you Detective Trueblood?"

"Please call me Jace. And I'm the Lieutenant, Chief of Detectives at the department," Jace acknowledged. "I heard that you're a doctor. A pediatric surgeon."

"I am. As was my father before me." Jackson took a sip of his wine. "And, please, feel free to call me Jackson." Breaking a roll in half, he buttered one side. "Were there other detectives in your family?"

Jace cut a small wedge from his steak as he shook his head. "No. I'm the first. My father built houses, the third generation of carpenters. When I was younger, I thought I'd follow in his footsteps, but life took me on another path." He shrugged. "But I do like to work with wood and make things with my hands. In fact, I've been remodeling a large Georgian Colonial here in Havendale."

"That sounds like quite an undertaking," Jackson said.

"Actually, I thought you and your wife would like to see the house. It will be Mibs' home after we're married." Since things seemed to be progressing without any significant problems, Jace asked, "Would you join us for dessert and coffee after dinner? I'm sure there are more questions you'd like to ask about the life Mibs has been living."

Jackson had started to lift a forkful of food; setting it back down on his plate, he glanced at Mibs, then turned back to Jace. "Yes, I would like to see the house. And I would like to hear everything about her life, everything she is willing to tell us." He reached for his water glass, took a sip, then glanced toward Mibs again.

A loud scream pierced the air, interrupting the conversation.

Jace pushed his chair back and stood, automatically turning toward the sound.

Before he could move away from the table, a member of the waiting staff rushed through the door. "Detective Trueblood. I saw you come in earlier. I…I think we need some help out there. *I* saw it all!"

"Calm down," Jace instructed. "Tell me what's happening." Jace listened as the young man excitedly told the story from his viewpoint.

"A couple had been sharing a meal in the corner of the restaurant. This agitated man marched up to their table. He yelled, 'Susan! What are you doing? I came home from work and found a teenager babysitting our kids.' Taking a deep breath, the waiter continued. 'The guy seemed really angry and kept yelling. 'People told me that you were cheating on me, but I didn't want to believe them.'

"The woman tells him, 'Bill, you're always

working. Then, you're too tired to go out when you get home. So why should I be stuck in the house all the time?'

"'I don't keep you chained to the house,' the guy, this Bill, said, 'There are a lot of things you could do and places you could go without meeting another man!' I saw it all," the waiter repeated, then continued. "Suddenly, Bill grabbed a steak knife from the table and yanked his wife from her chair. Pulling her, this Susan, against his chest, he held the knife to her throat and threatened her. 'If you no longer want to be my wife, just say so. I can take care of that right now!'"

Jace held up his hand to stop the waiter's recitation as he headed for the doorway. "Call 911."

"I think the *maître d'* already called them." The waiter gulped for air.

"Call them back. Tell them there's an officer on the premises and to come in silent."

As he entered the main dining room, a terrified woman, held tightly by a middle-aged man, had a knife to her throat. The man was backed up against the table; more hurt than anger was etched across his face. Jace noticed another guy at the table. Perspiration dripped from the second man's forehead as he leaned away from the knife-wielding Bill.

Jace inched towards the table, used a calm voice, and deployed various phrases he'd learned in hostage negotiation training. "Bill," Jace addressed the husband. "I can tell you're upset, but I don't reckon you really wanna hurt

Susan. Let's go somewhere, and we can talk about this problem."

"Talk about it?" Bill's voice cracked with emotion. "There's nothing to talk about. I work two jobs to give her all the stuff she wants. This is how she repays me?"

Susan gasped when the edge of the knife pricked her skin. A tiny drop of blood appeared, sliding down her pale neck.

"What about your kids, Bill? What will happen to them if their mother isn't around?"

Jace took a small step closer, casually positioning his hands on his hips. Having his hands there, he put his fingers within a few inches of his gun. Jace tried to keep Bill from feeling threatened while also preparing to stop the man if needed. "Bill, if you kill your wife, you will go to prison. The kids won't have a mom or a dad. Are you gonna do that to them?" He nodded to Susan and gave her a disdainful glare. "Is a cheatin' wife worth it? Is she worth losin' your freedom and your kids?"

Bill stared at Jace for several long, drawn-out moments. He slowly lowered the knife from his wife's neck and released his hold on her. Susan stumbled away, clutching her throat. A paramedic, who had arrived with the police and had been quietly standing by, moved her away.

"That was a good decision, Bill." Jace held out his hand. "Why don't you give me the knife?"

The man's anger seemed to collapse as he slowly handed the weapon to Jace. As soon as the knife was in Jace's hand, a police officer stepped up and secured handcuffs on Bill.

Jace placed his hand on the man's shoulder.

"Go with him, Bill. I'll be there in a bit."

The other guy, who'd been frozen in fright with his mouth hanging open, gulped loudly. As soon as the agitated husband had been led away, he suddenly became brave. "I'm going to press charges!" he exclaimed. The man scanned the room until he spotted Susan being treated for her minor wound. He added, "I'll talk Susan into pressing charges too."

Jace shook his head. "I suppose you could do that, but I don't think you should."

"Why not?" the guy's chin jutted out.

"Because if you do, I'm going to charge you with inciting violence."

"Inciting violence? What are you talking about?"

"The only reason that guy came here and caused this problem is because you were threatening the well-being of his family and home." Turning his back on the man, Jace directed Bill's wife to come closer.

When Susan approached, Jace frowned. "I was raised to believe that marriage is a sacred thing. You should try to work things out. But, if you aren't fixin' to be faithful to your husband, then, in my opinion, you should get a divorce and be done with it."

Susan cast her eyes down. "I never thought...I never meant..." she sputtered. "May I go now?"

"You need to give a statement before you leave." Jace nodded toward a waiting policewoman.

The man remaining at the table fumbled with his wallet and tossed some bills down. As the man stood to leave, Jace held a hand up, stopping him.

"From the part of the country I come from, they have a sayin' about a varmint who tries to poach another man's wife." Jace leaned close and quietly mumbled something to the man.

Jace made sure no one else could hear his words, but they caused the man's face to turn beet red and a flicker of uncertainty to flash in his eyes. He cautiously slid past Jace and hurried out of the restaurant.

The paramedics began packing their gear. The other guests in the dining area turned their attention to their meals, excitedly murmuring to each other. And the owner of the restaurant rushed to Jace's side.

"Lieutenant Trueblood, thank you! Thank you!" Raphael Pascal gushed. "*Oh, mon Dieu!* That situation could have turned out so much worse if you hadn't persuaded that man to give you the knife." Pascal clasped his hands together and held them to his chest. "How can I ever repay you? I should give you free meals anytime. Come anytime. Be my guest."

"That's not necessary." Jace shook his head emphatically. "It wouldn't be appropriate for me to accept any gifts or compensation for doing my job," Jace insisted.

Heading back to his table and the members of his dinner party, Jace found Mibs waiting in the doorway. Mr. and Mrs. Richmond stood behind her. They had witnessed the action which had just taken place.

Mibs hugged Jace's arm, placing her head on his shoulder. He winked at her and said,

"Everything's fine, sweetheart."

"Nicely done, Lieutenant," Jackson said.

Jace brushed off the compliment. "Sometimes domestic disputes can be a problem, but most of the time, a little talkin' can calm things down."

By the time they reached the table, Raphael Pascal was hovering by Jace. "Your food must be cold now, Lieutenant. I'll have a fresh dish brought out."

"No, thank you. I have to go down to the police station." Jace could tell that Pascal would be disappointed if he didn't let him reciprocate somehow. So he made a request. "Mr. Pascal, I have asked that we have desserts boxed to take home with us. Would you make sure they are ready when my guests leave?"

"Oh! *Mais oui*, Lieutenant Trueblood. I will see to it personally." Pascal clasped his hands together again and scurried off to the kitchen.

"Do you think you will be at the station very long?" Mibs asked.

"Shouldn't take long. I would have someone else handle it, but I told the guy I'd talk to him. I need to keep my word. One of the patrol cars is waiting outside to give me a ride." Leaning down, Jace slipped his credit card into Mibs' hand. "Sweetheart, take care of the bill with this card. Sign it as Jace E. Trueblood. You shouldn't need my PIN, but if you do...." Jace pulled out his small notepad, tore out a sheet, wrote four numbers on it, and handed it to Mibs. "Mr. Richmond is agreeable to coming by the house after dinner, so I'll meet you there."

Jace straightened and surveyed the small

group. "Please, enjoy your meal, and I'll join you later."

Jace glanced at Tony, "Tony, would you tell the Richmonds how to get to my home and give Mibs a hand until I get there?"

"Sure thing. Go do what you need to do."

"Jace," Jackson Richmond piped up. "I'll take care of the bill for the meal."

"Thanks for the offer, but it's already covered. Just relax and visit."

~~

Pascal escorted the dinner group to the restaurant's front door when they were ready to leave, all the while extolling compliments about the abilities and bravery of Lieutenant Trueblood.

He patted Mibs' hand. "You have a lovely family. Please bring them back soon."

"Thank you, Mr. Pascal. The food was wonderful."

Chapter 27

An hour later, Jace was dropped off at his home by a patrol car. He let himself in and found his newly extended family in the living room. Apparently, they had spent the last hour enjoying desserts, coffee, and champagne while visiting around the dining room table. Then, they moved to the couch and chairs in the living room as they continued their conversations.

Aunt Bernie occupied a mission oak rocking chair next to the refurbished stone fireplace. Tony sat on a dining room chair, which he had brought into the room. Seeing that Mibs and Camilla were snuggled between Mr. and Mrs. Richmond on the new leather couch made Jace glad that he'd purchased the more extended version of the sofa. Lawrence appeared relaxed in the matching recliner.

"I'll grab you a chair," Tony said when he saw Jace standing in the doorway.

"Thanks, Tony. I'll get myself some coffee."

"Jace," Mibs said, "Mr. Pascal sent an entire meal for you. It's in the refrigerator if you're hungry."

Jace shrugged. "I'll probably save it for tomorrow. Right now, I reckon I'd like a cup of black coffee and maybe some of the chocolate cake if there's any left."

"Trueblood, sit down," Tony directed. "You've been busy. I'll get your coffee and cake."

Jace removed his suit jacket and hung it on the chair's back. He noticed that Camilla eyed the nine-millimeter automatic clipped to his belt with an uncertain expression. A gun had been a part of his lawman's attire for many years; Jace often forgot that it sometimes made others uncomfortable. He unclipped the pistol and placed it behind an antique wooden clock on the fireplace mantel.

After removing his gun, Jace sat. He listened as Mibs shared some of what they had been discussing. Mibs told him that she had described the opening of Monahan's Sewing Shop to her parents. Jackson Richmond had shared the story about a heart operation he'd recently done on a two-year-old toddler. Camilla had talked about the apprenticeship in engineering she'd just started.

Although he sensed that there was still an aura of unfamiliarity and uncertainty between the gathered people, Jace was pleased to see that everyone seemed eager to get to know each other.

Jace found out that Mibs had invited Crystal and Camilla to join her for the planned weekend search for the perfect wedding dress.

From the expression of joy that filled Crystal's face, Jace could tell that the invitation meant a lot to Mibs' mother. Anna, his mother, would fly to Havendale the day before the trip and accompany Mibs to Metrofield. Crystal and Camilla would meet them at the bridal shop where Whitney and her mother had arranged the first appointment.

"You know what might be nice?" Lawrence said. "I think there's a football game that Saturday; us guys could go to that." He turned to his father. "Pop, if you haven't promised your box seats to one of your friends that day, Jace could bring his father so we could meet him; make a day of it. What do you think?"

"That's a good suggestion," Jackson responded. He turned toward Jace. "That is if you'd like to do that. We are very pleased to have found our missing daughter." Jackson shifted his focus to Mibs. "But we don't want to suddenly push ourselves into her life."

Jace also regarded Mibs. He realized she had been listening to the conversation. Meeting his questioning glance, she gave a slight nod.

Jace had spent a good bit of time the other day discussing what Mibs thought and how she felt about the situation–finding out that she had been born into a wealthy family, had been kidnapped when she was a baby, been rescued from a garbage bin in a trash-strewn alley, and then raised by a loving senior citizen. He knew that Mibs didn't want to give up the life she had. However, she also wanted to know about her lost family. She had told him that it wasn't her biological family's fault that she had been apart from them for all these years. But now, she was who she was. That wouldn't change. Mibs' words had renewed his pride in the woman she had become.

"I think that would work. I'll call my dad and see if he is free." Jace ran his hand through his hair as he considered the offer.

"And you too, Tony," Lawrence added. "You're welcome to join us."

Tony rubbed his chin. "I'm afraid I will be on the west coast that weekend. I'm in the process of finishing details for a new video game." Tony reached over to squeeze Aunt Bernie's hand. "But, I'll make sure Aunt Bernie has Zoom up and running. In fact, I'll make sure my cousin, Luca, is available if she has any computer problems."

"That would be great, Tony," Mibs said. "I want to make sure that Aunt Bernie is there, even if it is virtually. I want her opinion before I make a final decision about my wedding dress." Turning to her aunt, Mibs asked, "Marge and Hazel are planning on being there with you, aren't they, Aunt Bernie?"

"Yes, they are. They plan to spend much of the weekend with me. They're excited about watching the activity on the computer."

Jace noticed the fatigue in Bernie's expression. "Considerin' that it's after 9:00, maybe you would like to call it a night."

Bernie gave him a grateful smile. "Maybe that would be a good idea." She glanced at Tony. "Anthony, would you have time to give me a ride? Jace can bring Mibs home after everyone else has left."

"Of course, I always have time for my best girl." Tony stood and handed Bernie her cane.

A short time later, the Richmonds decided that it was time to leave. Camilla promised to bring her family by Monahan's Sewing Shop before flying home the next day. They wanted to see Mibs' and Bernie's place of business.

It didn't take Jace and Mibs long to clean up the dishes from the dining room and put away the few pieces of dessert which remained.

"It appears as if you have enough dessert for a day or two." Mibs packaged up the last piece of cake and two apple tarts, storing them in the refrigerator.

"Actually, I'll probably eat those little apple pies for breakfast and have the cake after dinner tomorrow."

"You do like your sweets, don't you?" Mibs chuckled.

Jace gave her a crooked grin, grabbing her around the waist and pulling her onto his lap as he sat back on a kitchen stool. "I definitely like sweets." He ran his thumb across her lips. "And you're my favorite sweet thing."

Jace felt Mibs take a quick breath before she leaned forward and lightly kissed him. Her lips barely touched his. Soft. Like butterfly wings. His mind slowed, and he had to remind himself to breathe. That gentle kiss affected him almost as much as a more prolonged, deeper kiss would have.

A loud chirp interrupted the romantic moment.

"Ahh! Not now," Jace grumbled as the cell phone rang again.

Mibs sighed, slipped out of his embrace, and retrieved her phone from the counter. "It's Aunt Bernie. I should answer."

After listening for a moment, Mibs said, "I'll bring it with me. I should be home shortly."

"Everything okay?" Jace placed his hand on her back.

"Aunt Bernie left her purse here. She asked me to bring it home."

Mibs found the small clutch purse on the floor near the rocker Bernie had occupied. As she scooped it up, Jace reached toward the weapon he'd slid behind the clock earlier. Changing his mind, he left it there.

"I shouldn't need my gun just to drive over to your house."

"Wouldn't think so," Mibs agreed. "Of course, you probably have that .38 Special in the ankle holster attached to your leg."

Jace winked. "Seldom leave home without it." Pausing, he thought about the registered firearms he owned. "I'm going to buy another gun lockbox, maybe even a gun safe."

"I know you already have a lockbox upstairs, and you said your rifle is unloaded and locked in the upstairs closet." Mibs tilted her head as she considered his words. "Are you thinking they should be more secure than that?"

"What I'm thinking, my dear wife-to-be, is about the possibility that the Lord may bless us with children. If in the not-too-distant future, we have young'uns runnin' around, I have to consider their safety." He took Mibs' hand in his. "I need to get in the habit *now* of securing my guns as soon as I enter the house. If it becomes a routine before we have kids, then when and if we do, it will be automatic."

Mibs leaned forward and kissed him on the cheek. "You will be a great parent."

A few minutes later, Jace and Mibs climbed into his Silverado. The temperature had dropped significantly through the evening. Jace let the truck idle for a few minutes, giving the engine a chance to warm up. A sprinkling of snowflakes began to fall, gathering on the windshield momentarily before the blast of the heater melted them. Delicate, white crystals disappeared after a brief appearance on the warming glass.

Mibs shivered. She pulled her cloth cloche hat out of her coat pocket and settled it on her head. "Jace, maybe you should have a hat too. That cold wind is picking up."

Reaching over the seat, he rummaged through a plastic container. When he pulled his arm forward, he held a stocking cap with the Havendale Police Department logo on the front. "Is that better?" he asked as he pulled on the cap with HPD embroidered across the front.

"It may not go with the fancy suit you're wearing tonight, but it should definitely keep your head warm."

Jace's police-issue phone rang through the truck's hand-free device just as he started to back out of the driveway. He threw the vehicle back into park and pushed the answer button.

"Trueblood. How can I help you?"

Chapter 28

As Jace listened, his brow wrinkled, and sorrow filled his face. "I'll be right there."

"Not again," he mumbled as he disconnected. Jace leaned toward Mibs and touched his forehead to hers. "There has been another accident involving teens."

"Oh, no!" Mibs gasped. "Is it bad?"

"Yeah, it's bad," Jace affirmed as he straightened back up. He repeated what the officer had told him. "There were four kids in the car. Three of them have minor injuries." The emotion flowed into his words as he added, "One of them is trapped in the car. He's seriously hurt, and they aren't sure if they will be able to cut him out in time." He paused. "I'll take you home, then head to the scene."

"Wait," Mibs demanded. "Where is the accident?"

"Just inside the city limits, Fenton Street, by the old shoe factory."

"That's the opposite way from my house. You'll lose at least ten minutes if you take me home first. Head to Fenton. I can wait."

"Are you sure, sweetheart?"

"Just go, honey. Go."

Jace stopped long enough to reach under his seat, pull out a LED light strip, and slap it onto the dashboard. He turned on the flashing blue and red light as he sped down the street. Reaching the accident scene, Jace skidded to a stop between an ambulance and a police cruiser. He jumped out of the truck and hurried over to the wrecked car.

Officer Brett Clarkson stepped forward as Jace approached. "Lieutenant." Clarkson guided Jace away from the driver's door of the vehicle. "I'm glad you're here. Can you get a number to call the trapped boy's parents? I think they will want to come here instead of waiting to meet us at the hospital."

"Talk to me. Tell me, what's going on?"

"The fire department has already cut the door open, but they're waiting for the emergency people to decide about proceeding further." The creases on Clarkson's coffee-colored skin deepened as he relayed the rest of the information. "They're trying to get an emergency doctor here to make a final decision."

"What kind of decision? Spell it out, Brett," Jace instructed.

"The EMT guys believe that the only thing that's kept the boy alive this long is the fact that the steering wheel is jammed so tightly against his lower waist that it's clamped the arteries. They think that once they pull him loose, he'll bleed out in seconds."

"Oh, no!" The thought of another young person dying felt like a stab in Jace's heart. "Have we identified the boy?"

Clarkson nodded. "His name is George Young, lives on Ninth Street."

"George Young," Jace mumbled. "I know him. He and his family go to my church."

Stepping back, Jace rubbed the back of his neck. "I'll see if I can get hold of his folks."

After calling dispatch and having them text the Young's phone number and address, Jace motioned to two uniformed officers waiting patiently by their squad car. He gave them the address on Ninth Street and told them to head in that direction but wait before pulling into the street until he called them.

Jace's call to those parents was one of the most difficult ones he'd ever made. Before he hung up, Jace told Mary and Rob Young that a police car would be pulling up. It would bring them directly to the scene.

He slipped the cell phone back into his pocket, then directed Clarkson to radio the dispatched squad car and have the officers pull up to Young's house.

Jace made his way back to the driver's side of the smashed Toyota. A member of the emergency personnel was leaning into the car, checking George's vitals. When the man stepped back, Jace tapped him on the shoulder.

"Could I talk to the boy?" Jace asked as he held out a slim wallet, open, showing his official identification.

After glancing at the ID, the technician nodded and stepped aside.

"Hello, George. I don't know if you remember me. I see you at church sometimes. I know your parents."

The boy's gray eyes focused on Jace. Eyes, which Jace remembered as bright and lively, now seemed glazed and pale. "Yeah, I recognize you. You're that detective, Lieutenant Trueblood. Right?"

"How y'all holdin' up, George?" Jace reached

out and placed his hand firmly on the teen's shoulder. He could smell the liquor; he knew the boy had been drinking. *'Lord,'* Jace thought to himself, *'he doesn't deserve this.'*

"I'm not hurting. In fact, I don't feel anything below my chest." The boy's chin quivered. He turned away for a brief moment. When he turned back, he said, "Lieutenant, sir, I'm sorry. I'm sorry I wrecked the car. Are you going to give me a ticket?"

Jace gave a snigger of disbelief when he heard the question. "I'm not worried about givin' anybody a ticket, son. I just want you to know everyone here is doing their best to take care of you."

"Lieutenant Trueblood, you wouldn't lie to me, would you? Will you be honest with me?"

Jace heard the sincerity in the boy's words. Squeezing the teen's shoulder, he promised, "I won't lie to you, George."

"Then, tell me...." George tried to take a deep breath. "Are my friends all right? Did I... did anyone get hurt?"

"Cuts and bruises mostly," Jace answered. "A boy appears to have a broken arm. But none of them seem to have any serious injuries."

George nodded. Peering squarely into Jace's eyes, he asked, "Sir, am I going to die?"

Jace forced himself not to break eye contact with the teen. He swallowed hard, trying to find the right words to answer him.

"You promised that you'd be honest," George reminded.

"I don't want you to give up hope, George." Jace cleared his throat. "But I was told that your chances are not good."

The gray eyes didn't waver. George's lips formed a sad smile. "Thank you, Lieutenant."

Jace leaned back, bending his knees and squatting on his haunches. He kept one hand on George's arm.

"Lieutenant," the boy's voice seemed weaker. "Do you think Father Smith would come and give me The Last Rights?"

"I'll call him for you, George. I'll call him right now," Jace assured him. Hearing a squad car pull up, he turned to see Mr. and Mrs. Young exit the cruiser and hurry forward. "But how about you talk to your parents for now?"

"They're here? Mom and Dad are here?"

Jace stepped back as the Youngs reached the car.

"We're here, son," Jace heard Rob Young say.

Jace stepped away and pulled out his cell phone, and found the number for the rectory. Then, motioning to the officers who'd just pulled in with the Youngs, he directed, "I need you to make another run. I need you to pick up the priest at Christ the King Church."

After reaching Father Smith and relaying the sad information, Jace glanced toward his truck. Not seeing Mibs through the windshield, Jace quickly surveyed the area. He caught sight of a sky-blue coat with a white collar. Even though she had her back to him, he knew it was Mibs. She stood near two of the injured teens as they leaned against the open door of the ambulance. A boy was lying on a stretcher inside the vehicle. Mibs and the girls seemed to be praying together.

By the time Jace maneuvered around the various vehicles, the girls were loaded into an ambulance. Mibs was left alone. She stepped back and bumped into Jace.

"Oh!" Mibs turned. "Oh, hi, honey," she said. "Umm, I didn't stay in the truck because I saw those teens, and … well, they seemed so forlorn, so scared."

Jace shook his head and smiled to himself. "Finding you giving comfort to someone does not surprise me at all. It's who you are." He reached for Mibs' hand and noticed the blood on the sleeve and front of her coat. "Sweetheart, I'm bettin' you gave those kids hugs because you got blood on your coat. I know it's your favorite coat."

Examining the stains, Mibs shrugged. "It's just a coat. Right now, it doesn't seem that important."

The emergency room doctor they'd been waiting for arrived just as the police car returned with Father Smith. Before the doctor or the priest could reach the crushed car, a cry of anguish pierced the night. Jace didn't have to ask; he knew it was Mary Young's voice. George had passed away.

Jace stood frozen in place, gritting his teeth. Mibs clung to his arm.

Finally, Jace said, "We brought in the guy making the fake identification cards, but there are probably quite a few of those fake IDs still out there. The kids can still use them to buy alcohol."

Determination filled his eyes as he continued. "I'm going to contact the principal at the high school and ask him to call an assembly for all the high school classes. I've gotta talk some sense into these kids. Maybe we can arrange a mock crash at the school and let the students get a better idea of the reality of these kinds of accidents." Shaking his head, Jace muttered, "Hell! I drank my share of beer when I was a teen. Even snuck some of my grandad's whiskey a few times. But I never...*never* got behind the wheel of a vehicle when I drank."

Mibs held his arm tighter, letting him vent his anger.

"I remember one night. I wasn't quite eighteen. I was partying with some buddies. Started drinkin'. I was drunk enough to almost convince myself that I could drive myself home. I stood there swaying, lookin' at my car keys for five minutes. Finally, I chucked those keys into the weeds and started walking home. I was two hours into that three-hour walk when a truck pulled up beside me and stopped."

"Was it someone you knew?" Mibs asked.

Jace nodded. "It was my dad. I have no idea if someone called him or if he just got worried 'cause I hadn't gotten home yet. He asked where the car was. I told him about deciding to toss the keys and walk. I thought he'd be fit to be tied and really lay into me. But Dad just said that it was a wise decision not to drive drunk. Told me to get in. I did. He didn't say another word the rest of the way home." Jace gave Mibs one of his half-smiles. "I got up late the next day, and the car was in the driveway. Both sets of keys were on the key hook inside the kitchen door. He must have gotten someone to drive him over, then spent some time searching through those weeds to find the keys." Jace shook his head. "He never mentioned that incident again."

"I've never noticed you drinking much," Mibs said.

"I still like a cold beer on a hot day or a glass of wine with a good meal. But I promised myself that I'd never get drunk like that again." Jace put his arm around Mibs and started toward the truck. "And I never have."

When Jace and Mibs reached his truck, Jace turned to stare at the accident scene. "I doubt if there is anything more I can do now. I'd best get you home, darlin'."

Taking a minute to wave and get an officer's attention, Jace told him that he would return shortly.

"Jace," Mibs said as she buckled her seatbelt. "It would be nice to think that everyone has someone to call for a ride if they realized they've drunk too much, but that isn't always true."

"I reckon you're right." Jace could tell that Mibs had something on her mind. "What are you thinking?"

"What if a local teenager realizes that they had too much to drink and didn't have a parent or friend who could pick them up? What if they could get...well, kind of a 'free pass' from the police."

"A free pass?" Jace's eyebrows lifted in question as he studied Mibs. "You mean, call a cop to pick them up?"

"Yes." Mibs crossed her arms, and she nodded. "They call, say they're in no shape to drive, then a police officer gives them a ride. No questions asked. No lectures. Just get safely home."

"Hmm." Jace considered the idea Mibs had presented as he watched the thin layer of ice on the windshield melt from the heater's blast of warm air. "That's a good idea, Mibs. I can clear it with the captain and send an email out. Make sure all the personnel at the station know. I can give out the non-emergency number at the school assembly."

"Maybe you could have a small article put in the local newspaper and on the social media section of the town's webpage," Mibs suggested.

Jace nodded in affirmation.

Carefully backing up before making a U-turn, Jace drove slowly away from Fenton Street.

Mibs pulled a rosary out of her purse. "Jace, I'm going to say a decade of the rosary for George's soul. Do you mind if I pray out loud?"

"I don't mind at all. I'll even pray with you."

Chapter 29

The next several weeks went by quickly. Mibs had a wonderful time during the wedding-dress-hunt weekend. Anna Trueblood and Crystal Richmond were more than cordial to each other. Mibs suspected that they would become good friends. When she stepped out of the dressing room and in front of the triple-mirrored area where Whitney, Camilla, and the moms were waiting, Mibs felt like a model on display. It was especially nice that Tony had given them a large monitor for Bernie's Zoom call. The picture was so clear that Mibs didn't have to ask Aunt Bernie what she thought. She could read her expression on the screen.

After trying on and rejecting half a dozen gowns, Mibs became a little disillusioned. The dresses were beautiful, but they just weren't what she wanted. However, when Mibs slipped into a long-sleeved, satin, full-skirted dress with a sheer silk overlay, she knew that *this* was the dress. The sheer sleeves were adorned with crystal-and-rose-embroidered appliques. Geometric crystal beading and embroidery covered the scalloped bodice. The soft silk overlay carried the same white rose design down the front of the skirt and around the hem. The dress fit perfectly. Mibs didn't think even a stitch of alteration would be needed. It was made for her.

After allowing the shop's sales assistant to

position the veil, she'd chosen–a waist-length, silk, lace veil attached to a half-circle of white silk rosebuds–Mibs slowly stepped out of the dressing room. She held her breath as she rejoined the gathered ladies: Anna Trueblood, Crystal and Camilla Jackson, Jeanette and Whitney Morgan, and of course, Aunt Bernie watching virtually on the computer scene.

Mibs stepped onto the small stage in front of the mirrors and studied her reflection. *Yes. Yes*, she thought to herself. *I do like this dress.* Turning around, she looked at the faces in front of her. The momentary silence was suddenly broken by several voices chattering at once.

"Beautiful!" Jeanette exclaimed.

Anna clasped her hands together as she smiled and nodded.

"You're lovely," Crystal said.

Camilla slowly walked around Mibs. "This dress is perfect."

Mibs moved directly in front of the computer screen. "Aunt Bernie, what do you think?"

On the screen, Aunt Bernie leaned forward, watching the activity taking place many miles away from Havendale. Hazel and Marge could be seen peeking over her shoulders. "My dear, you are beautiful." Giving a nod of approval, Bernie said, "Unless you want to continue trying on more dresses, I would agree that this one is perfect."

After eyeing the softly flowing wedding gown with pleasure, the tall, exuberant Whitney faced her best friend. "Mibs, I can tell by the sparkle in your eyes that you absolutely love this dress. I'm right, aren't I?"

Mibs smiled widely as she slowly nodded. "I really do love it," she said before the smile faded and a hint of uncertainty eclipsed her eyes. Mibs leaned toward the sales specialist who'd been assisting her. She motioned to the woman. Mibs waited until she was close.

"Before I make a definite decision, I need to know the cost of this gown. I didn't see a price, but I did see the tag, which listed the designer. This particular designer is very well known. I'm afraid one of her gowns may be more than I have budgeted for my wedding dress."

"Oh!" the woman exclaimed, not making any effort to keep her voice low. "I was told not to allow you to see any prices. My understanding is that you are not to pay for your gown. I was told to let you pick any wedding dress you desired."

"What?" Mibs' mouth fell open. "Who....then, is paying for it?"

Anna Trueblood stepped forward and patted Mibs' hand. "We all are." When Mibs' eyes widened in wonder, Anna explained, "Bernie, Crystal, Jeanette, and I are sharing the cost of this entire shopping trip."

"Uh-huh." The colorful bangle bracelets on Jeanette's arm jangled as she propped her hands on her hips. "That's right."

With a hopeful tone in her voice, Crystal said, "Please let us do this."

It took Mibs a moment to find her voice. Then, she looked at the image on the computer monitor. "Aunt Bernie?" she questioned.

"Mibs, sometimes the best thing to do when offered a gift is to accept it gracefully."

After seeing the pleased smile on her great-aunt's face, Mibs turned toward the extended family gathered around her. In the past, Aunt Bernie had been her only family. Now, she was surrounded by a group of women who cared about her. A lump caught in her throat. She had to swallow a couple of times before she could say, "Thank you."

~~

After that weekend, the days leading up to the wedding seemed to pass even faster. On February 13th, Bernice Monahan found herself resting on a cushioned bench in a classroom at Christ the King's grade school. She watched Whitney and Mib's soon-to-be mother-in-law, Anna Trueblood, flutter around Mibs, adding last-minute touches. Positioning the veil. Adjusting the hem of the bridal gown. Mibs' friends Tegan, Olivia, and Sophie had not only beautifully decorated the church community center for the reception, but they'd also transformed a corner of the assigned classroom into a bride-prep area. Bernice felt a twinge of nostalgia as thoughts of Mibs as a baby, a young child, a teenager, and then a self-assured young adult swirled through her mind. So much had happened in the last few years. Life as she'd known it had changed. But that is the way it should be. Change is part of life, part of God's plan.

Bernice watched Mibs turn away from the mirror and step toward her. "Aunt Bernie, are you ready?"

Her heart filled with love for the beautiful bride who stood in front of her. Mibs was no longer her little girl. She'd grown into a beautiful woman whom she'd be giving away in a few minutes to a very good man. As Bernice grabbed her cane and stood, her thoughts turned to prayer. *Dear Lord, thank you for letting me live long enough to raise Mibs. Thank You for letting me be her mother all these years. And thank you for helping me teach her to love You.*

"I'm ready," Bernice said. She'd had a long, heart-filled talk with Mibs the night before. The years of love they'd shared were permanently etched into each of their hearts. There was no need for added words now.

"I better go into the church. It's time for me to be seated," Anna declared, grabbing her purse and hurrying out of the classroom.

The silky fabric of Whitney's dress swished as she picked up Mibs' bouquet as well as her own. The fun-loving, ebony-skinned beauty who'd become Mibs' best friend during their shared college days released a contented sigh. "I'm so happy for you, Mibs."

"Thank you for everything, Whitney. I'm lucky to have you by my side."

"I know," Whitney playfully responded. "We're lucky to have each other as friends." She carefully gathered the back hem of Mibs' wedding gown with her free hand, intending to make sure it didn't pick up a speck of dust on their way across the lawn to the church. Even though it was a cold day, they'd decided to forgo putting coats on for the short walk from the school.

Mibs held her arm out to her aunt. Bernie leaned on Mibs with one hand and used her other to hold onto her cane for support. When they reached the vestibule, Whitney went in first. The music started as she stepped down the aisle.

Bernice proudly stood by Mibs as they waited for the bride's song to begin. Even if she hadn't already realized that Mibs loved Jace, Bernice would have been able to tell as she held her girl's arm. Bernice felt Mibs' pulse increase and saw true joy on her face as she gazed toward the young man waiting for her at the end of the aisle.

Chapter 30

Jace and Juan had stepped out of the sacristy and moved to their appointed spot in front of the altar. Jace was surprised by how full the church was. He noticed the detectives and quite a few officers from the station among the group. Scanning the pews, he saw Captain Taylor and his wife. Jace smiled when the captain gave him a quick salute. A flicker of movement toward the back of the nave caught his attention. He realized his mother had just entered and was being escorted by Tony to the front seat. Anthony Vitali and Brice Long served as ushers, smartly dressed in tuxedos. Jace winked at his mom when she reached the pew. She blew him a kiss. His dad proudly occupied the seat next to her. Jace was pleased that several of his relatives and friends had made the trip from Tennessee. Across the aisle, the Richmond family shared a long pew with Bernie's friends, Marge and Hazel. Jeanette and Leroy Morgan sat directly behind them.

"Juan," Jace asked nervously, "you have the ring?"

"Yes, I have the ring," Juan rolled his eyes as he answered. "You've been Mr. Calm and Cool all morning. Now, you're getting nervous?"

Jace gave him a sheepish grin. "Maybe."

Father Smith, who'd been helping the altar boy set up for Mass, ambled across the marble-tiled floor and joined Jace and Juan. "Beautiful day for a wedding," he declared just as the soft music playing in the background stopped.

The notes of *Ave Maria* filled the church. Everyone stood and turned toward the back. Whitney's teal-green dress shimmered with each step as she regally moved down the aisle. As soon as the lovely maid of honor stepped to the left of the altar and stopped, the music changed to Bach's *Arioso*.

Jace was mesmerized by the woman he loved as she slowly walked toward him. The light was filtering through the stained-glass windows and reflecting off the bright white of her gown, bathing her in soft color. As Mibs stepped closer, Jace could have sworn that he saw sunlight dancing in her eyes.

Juan poked Jace in the side with his elbow. "Breathe, buddy," he whispered. "You don't want to pass out."

Jace glanced at Juan and took a deep breath before turning back to the vision gliding down the aisle. "I can't help it if she takes my breath away," he mumbled to his friend.

When they were barely a foot away, Bernie took Mibs' hand and placed it in his, smiling fondly at him. Jace leaned down and placed a kiss on the soft, white curls crowning the kind, aged woman's head.

"Thank you, Aunt Bernie."

Mibs took the last step to stand beside Jace, gazing into his face. Jace was sure his heart would melt when he saw all the love reflected back to him from her eyes.

They both turned forward as Father Smith began the opening prayer. "In the name of the

Father, and the Son, and the Holy Spirit."

~~

Captain Hank Taylor put his arm around his wife's shoulder as they stepped through the church doors after the wedding Mass. He smiled at Mr. and Mrs. Jace Trueblood as they greeted guests who filed by the receiving line at the back of the vestibule.

"They seem so happy," Cassandra Taylor commented to her husband.

"Yes, they do," Hank replied. But before he could say more, his cell phone vibrated.

He pulled the phone from his pocket and hit the button. "This is Taylor." His brows wrinkled, and his mouth turned to a frown as he listened. "I'll be right there."

"What is it?" Cassandra queried, noticing the troubled expression spread across Hank's face.

"We have an officer down," Hank sadly answered. He squeezed his wife's hand and suggested that she continue to the reception. "Don't say anything to Jace. Today isn't a day for him to worry about one of our team being shot. So do me a favor, Cass, and tell Brice and Juan that I want them to stay with the wedding party. I'll text them when I get details."

As Hank stepped around the gathered guests, he noticed that several of the members of the Havendale Police Department were checking their phones, then looking toward him. He nodded to each of them and motioned toward the side door.

With all the people and the traditional

activities that filled a wedding reception, Hank hoped that neither Jace nor Mibs would notice that a few of their guests were missing the reception.

~~

When the band started playing George Strait's 'I Cross My Heart,' Jace took Mibs' hand and led her to the dance floor. After sharing their first dance as husband and wife, the couple approached the table where the Richmond family was seated.

An expression of surprise and then delight filled Jackson Richmond's face when Mibs smiled at him. "I believe it's time for the father-daughter dance."

About the Author

Joan L. Kelly currently lives in Virginia and enjoys spending time with her daughters, sons-in-law, and especially her grandkids.

Stitch in the Ditch is the third in the *Mibs Monahan* Cozy Mystery Series. *A Thread of Evidence* is the first; *Notions of Murder* is the second.

Joan's philosophy is that life can often be difficult; fiction stories are excellent therapy. When life gets hard, escape for a while in a good book.

Previously published books, *My Big Feet, Hiding the Stranger,* and *The DNA Connection,* were written for younger readers.

Joan Kelly's YA work has been called "highly recommended for community library fiction collections" by *Midwest Book Review.*

Published by
Full Quiver Publishing
PO Box 244
Pakenham ON
K0A2X0
www.fullquiverpublishing.com

* 9 7 8 1 9 8 7 9 7 0 5 2 4 *